BOGBRUSH
the Barbarian

To the Parliament Street Writers' Group, of Parliament Street Library in Toronto, and especially to Vern, Simon and Laurie for their delusional belief that this is great literature.

Also to Bill Powell, who knows it isn't. — H.W.

KCP Fiction is an imprint of Kids Can Press

Text © 2010 Howard Whitehouse
Illustrations © 2010 Bill Slavin

Kids Can Press acknowledges the financial support of the Government of Ontario, through the Ontario Media Development Corporation's Ontario Book Initiative; the Ontario Arts Council; the Canada Council for the Arts; and the Government of Canada, through the BPIDP, for our publishing activity.

Published in Canada by
Kids Can Press Ltd.
29 Birch Avenue
Toronto, ON M4V 1E2

Published in the U.S. by
Kids Can Press Ltd.
2250 Military Road
Tonawanda, NY 14150

www.kidscanpress.com

Edited by Tara Walker
Designed by Marie Bartholomew

Manufactured in Louiseville, Qc, Canada, in 5/2010 by Transcontinental Printing

This book is printed on acid-free paper that is 100% ancient-forest friendly (100% post-consumer recycled).

CM 10 0 9 8 7 6 5 4 3 2 1

Library and Archives Canada Cataloguing in Publication

Whitehouse, Howard
    Bogbrush the barbarian / by Howard Whitehouse ;
with illustrations by Bill Slavin.

ISBN 978-1-55337-701-6 (bound)

I. Slavin, Bill II. Title.

PZ7.W537Bo 2010   j823'.92   C2010-900208-3

Kids Can Press is a *Corus*™ Entertainment company

BOGBRUSH

the Barbarian

Howard Whitehouse
Illustrated by Bill Slavin

Kids Can Press

TALK LIKE A BARBARIAN!

 Bogbrush speaks the way barbarian heroes are meant to. It's a mixture of *thous* and *thees* and odd, old-fashioned words that sound like Shakespeare as spoken by an idiot. You probably won't understand everything he says. Most people he meets don't know what he's talking about. Bogbrush himself doesn't really understand what he's saying half the time. Here are a few words of vocabulary that you will probably want to try out on the tough kids at school. Or not, your choice.

aye: yes

nay: no

ere: before

steed: a horse; possibly a donkey or a camel; probably not a goat

thews: muscles, always big; "mighty thew'd" is a phrase that gets used A LOT

thee, thou: you

hadst, hast: had, have

wouldst, couldst: would, could

forsooth: a medieval thing that medieval people said; I have no idea if it means anything

varlet, villain: a bad person

slay: to kill someone or something

cleave: to cut up with extra force

smite: to hit, usually leading to slaying and possibly cleaving (see above)

vanquish: to defeat, after all that smiting, cleaving and slaying

ho!: a generally useful sort of word that indicates you are going somewhere or have noticed something

What's a Barbarian, Anyway?

The ancient Greeks thought anyone who wasn't, er, Greek was a savage who spoke in noises like "ba-ba-ba." So that's where the word comes from. Nowadays we use it for wild, muscular, violent people from rugged lands with no proper plumbing who dress in furs and bits of chain mail and carry big axes. Not that you meet them every day.

Where and When Does this Stupid Tale Take Place?

You know "Once upon a time" and "Far, far away"? Around about then, and pretty close to there. Don't ask so many questions, kid.

AND NOW, ON WITH THE STORY!

PROLOGUE

(The bit that comes first.)

The July snow was blowing sideways across the frozen plain toward the village. The brief summer of the Northlands was still days away. Yet inside the log-walled settlement there was rejoicing. A new baby was to be named!

Villagers gathered in front of the ceremonial fire, wearing their best bear-furs, shining armor and weapons, and their finest helmets with horns. That was just the womenfolk. The men were dressed up as well. Someone had polished the skulls above the gateway that welcomed visitors. Everyone was drinking ale from huge flagons, although the children weren't allowed more than five cups of the thick, sticky brew. Whole oxen were roasted as snacks. You could eat as many turnips as you liked.

The naming ceremony took place in the temple, which still smelled of the cows who lived inside. For this special occasion, most of them had been moved outside. The old priest, an ancient figure draped in the pelt of a great wolf, with the teeth of a sabre-toothed cat around his neck, cackled to the assembled village. He was too old to talk and could only cackle.

"Grock brig giss wrooorrrkk figgle naaammigg hiierrkk? Hwurkgh!"

This meant something like "Who brings this child to be named?" Or possibly "I have swallowed the knucklebone of a goat and may choke if nobody helps me."

The villagers assumed it was the first of these sayings. A young yokel and his wife stepped forward. You could tell they were yokelfolk because they had straw in their hair, very few teeth and no armor at all.

WORD OF THE DAY: yokel — *an insulting term for someone who lives in the country, which suggests that he or she is uneducated and probably stupid.*

See how many of your schoolmates you can call a yokel before one of them smacks you in the head.

An old man, who had a massive bronze helmet with horns on either side and many swords, spears and axes — so many that he paid a boy to carry most of them — stepped forward as well. "I am the grandfather," he announced. "I shall name the wee lad."

He wasn't really a "wee lad" at all. His mother was straining under the weight of the babe, who was twice the size of every infant ever seen in the village. The older ladies had passed him to one another, each comparing him to prize-winning pigs they had owned. Nobody had ever hoisted a baby of such size.

The grandfather looked around, challenging all to argue with his right to name the boy. The baby's parents obviously weren't about to quarrel with a heavily armed grandpa.

"He shall be named Bogbrush, and he will become a mighty barbarian warrior. Like myself, of course."

"Bogbrush," whispered one of the old ladies at the back. "That's a nice name."

A MOMENT FOR EDUCATION:
Bogbrush *is British slang for a brush used to clean a bog.*

ANOTHER MOMENT FOR EDUCATION:
Bog *is British slang for a toilet. See also* loo *(page 398).*

The most muscle-bound of the village grand-mothers hoisted the infant, who burped loudly, and tossed him at the old priest; the holy man staggered as the baby flopped into his arms, and he began to cackle wildly yet again. The baby, now known as Bogbrush, threw up all over him.

"A mighty warrior shall he be," intoned the grandfather.

CHAPTER 1

(I'm holding up a finger.)

It was a perfect evening for monster slaying. Bogbrush, the mighty barbarian hero, was ready. He was hunched behind the barnyard wall, a gigantic sword gleaming in his huge fist. The night was dark, but not so dark that the warrior couldn't see his own feet; he recognized them both at the end of his legs. It was cool, so he wouldn't be sweaty, even with all the hacking and slashing he'd have to do. It was dry, which was good because nobody likes to be out in the rain, horrible man-eating creatures included. And tomorrow was laundry day, so his mother could get the monster blood out of his trousers.

He had only one pair, and his mother washed clothes just twice a year.

The young barbarian thought about all these things, one by one. He was a slow thinker. Big, blond, rippling with muscles, but not quick between the ears.

His grandfather, Bumrash, had been a great slayer of foul beasts, vile things from the marshes and the smaller, less athletic sorts of demon. The people of the village spoke of the old man, now dead, as a great swordsman, a mighty hero. He'd been killed by a snake when he was ninety-four; he didn't cook it properly and got food poisoning.

Bogbrush had heard the men talking about his grandfather.

"That Bumrash. He was an idiot as a boy. Later on, he grew into a lunatic," said old Bedsock.

"I remember him as a raving maniac," recalled Lardgut the Elder.

The young man didn't know exactly what it meant to be an idiot or a raving maniac, but he thought these were high compliments. His grandfather must have been greatly admired. And now he, Bogbrush, a boy of at least fifteen and maybe even eighteen summers (none of his family were good at counting), held the mighty sword once carried by Bumrash. The sword was called Headlopper because it was made for lopping. Heads, mostly, although Bogbrush was only allowed to practice on turnips. Still, the lad was ready for heads. Monster heads. Big monster heads. The kind with horns.

Suddenly a sound pierced the air. A terrible scream of evil. It went "Moooohh! Moooh!"

Bogbrush shivered with a jolt of fear but — being a mighty barbarian hero — he jumped up onto the wall. Headlopper was in his hand, the massive blade shining in the moonlight. He stared into the field and saw the bright (and clearly evil) eyes staring back. The monster had big savage horns with which to stab and gore and . . . stab and gore. There were probably other words for it, but

Bogbrush couldn't think of them. The vast beast paced fiercely, its wicked, poisonous breath making fog in the cold air. The moon disappeared behind a cloud. He had to strike now!

"I must cleave this foul thing in twain!" said Bogbrush to himself, but quite loudly. "I shall smite it ere it knoweth I am here!" Luckily, the monster showed no signs of understanding any of this. Almost nobody understood Bogbrush, exactly.

He always spoke as his grandfather had taught him — like a barbarian hero. He used complicated sentences full of important-sounding words, sometimes with strange *eths* on the end of them. It was hard for him to remember how to talk like this, and often he even confused himself.

WORD OF THE DAY: twain means *"in two pieces." Use it in conversation with your brother or sister, as in "I shall cleave this mushroom and sausage pizza in twain, and thou shalt choose which bit to take."*

The rest of his family (who, as you'll remember, were yokels) didn't even try to understand what Bogbrush meant when he said things like "I hadst closeth the pigsty ere bedtime, yet forsooth I hast forgeteth to shuteth yon gate!" They just followed the squeals of the pigs he had let loose in the flower beds.

Bogbrush leaped forward, sword in hand. The huge blade swung through the night, slashing into the monster's hide before the savage beast could strike against the hero. The fiendish creature toppled with a grunt.

CHAPTER 2

(I'm waving two fingers.)

Bogbrush was in trouble again. Big trouble. Bad trouble.

"That's another cow you've chopped into bits, Bogbrush," said his mother. "That's four. Or seven. A lot, anyway."

Bogbrush said that wasn't true at all. Two of the monsters he'd slain had been pigs.

"That makes no difference," said his father. "It weren't our cowses or pigses you've killed." You could tell Bogbrush's father was a yokel (and not a heroic barbarian warrior) by the way he talked. "I have to pay Old Stinkweed twenty pieces of silver, or fourteen, or something like that, for his cow. And there be the barn you burndid down —"

"That barn was full of demons!" said Bogbrush. "Vile devils. Inside the haystacks. Waiting to jump out and murder us all!"

"And the field of oats you trampled," said his mother.

COUNT LIKE A BARBARIAN! Bogbrush and his family have problems with numbers. You, too, can count like a hero from the frozen wastes! One, two, a lot, ten, more, nine — get the idea?

Bogbrush couldn't remember why or when he'd done that. He might have done it, though. It was exactly the kind of thing he spent his evenings and weekends doing. A hobby, really.

"So, we've decided it's time for you to leave home," said his parents together.

"Go on a quest?" said Bogbrush. "Seek my fortune with my bold sword and my undaunted courage?"

None of them knew what *undaunted* meant. Bogbrush had heard it somewhere. He thought it meant "bigger than a cucumber," but actually it doesn't.

WORD OF THE DAY: undaunted
means "not daunted," of course.
Look it up — you know how to
do that. Don't be daunted! Don't
be a silly dauntlehead!

"Arr!" said his father, which meant "yes."
"Yes," said his mother, which meant "arr!"

CHAPTER 3

(Waggling my thumb around as well.)

The whole village came out to see Bogbrush leave for his adventure. There was a strong opinion that the young man ought to seek his fortune in the sunny lands of the south, far, far away. People had brought gifts, many of them useful only in distant, tropical lands, like feathery fans or summer tunics with flowery prints. Mad Crockmind had made him a tiny window in a frame. "If it gets hot, you can open it and feel the breeze."

Bogbrush was dressed in his grandfather's helmet, a cloak of bearskin and a pair of boots sewn from walrus hide. He was bigger than Bumrash, so the old man's armor didn't fit, but his mother had used some of it to make a nice set of chain-mail underwear.

"Keep your personal bits safe," she told him. "You'll feel more confident."

He carried the sword, Headlopper, the axe, Nosebiter, and the famed spear, Gutjabber. He didn't bother with a shield. Shields were for sissies.

"Forsooth, mother. I have need of a steed!" said Bogbrush.

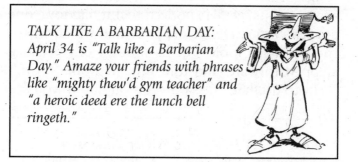

TALK LIKE A BARBARIAN DAY:
April 34 is "Talk like a Barbarian Day." Amaze your friends with phrases like "mighty thew'd gym teacher" and "a heroic deed ere the lunch bell ringeth."

"What's he sayin'?" whispered one of the old ladies. "I've never understood what he was talkin' about."

"An 'orse. A donkey. A goat," replied her friend, an even older lady. "Else he'll have to walk."

There was some grumbling that if Bogbrush had to walk, he might not get far enough away from the village before he changed his mind about going. The elders all muttered among themselves and decided to help their hero on his epic journey.

"We've bought you an 'orse," announced Lardgut the Elder, who was the village chief today. Everyone took turns being the village chief. They took turns being the village idiot as well.

It was, indeed, an 'orse, although not a very big one. It was a pony, one of those fat little creatures with long hair and stumpy legs that children like to ride. It was white with black spots. "Your mighty steed for questing," said Lardgut. Somebody giggled, but they were shut up in a hurry. The pony leaned forward and nibbled on one child's hat.

Bogbrush looked at the horse seriously. He examined its feet. He noticed that it had four, one at each corner. He looked at its tail, which was at the back. He looked at its mouth, but Bedsock stepped forward and told him to stop. "It ain't lucky to do that," he said. "It is our gift to you."

A MOMENT FOR EDUCATION: There is an old proverb, "Never look a gift horse in the mouth." People who know about horses can tell a horse's age by examining its teeth. So if someone gives you a horse as a present, it's rude to check whether your free gift is an elderly nag rather than a fine young mount.

Or maybe it's just good advice to avoid a nasty bite from a strange horse.

"I must name the fine stallion," said Bogbrush. "For he shall bear me toward deeds of valor."

"We call him Cuddles!" shouted a small child.

The crowd tried not to laugh; a lot of people pretended they were coughing.

"Nay," said Bogbrush. "'Tis not the name of the valiant mount of a hero." He thought for a moment. The veins on his forehead seemed to pop out, and his eyes crossed with the effort. He needed to think of a really impressive name for his steed. Something that would become part of the legend of the mighty Bogbrush.

"I shall call him Nobby!" declared Bogbrush. "Nobby shall be his name."

The young barbarian mounted his horse. Several people gasped as he threw one giant leg over the pony's back. "He'll crush the poor thing!" screamed a woman. He did not crush Nobby, thankfully, because both of his feet touched the ground. Bogbrush wasn't really sitting on the pony so much as crouching over it.

"Ho!" said Bogbrush as his father passed him the axe, the spear and a pouch of turnip sandwiches, his favorite. "I shall return once I have gained great treasure and a bold reputation."

"No need, dear," said his mother. "But write if you get the chance."

Bogbrush wouldn't have the chance, of course, because he didn't know how to write. But nobody in the village could read, so it had never been much of a problem.

WERD OV THE DAI: illiteracy — *whoops. Sorry. It was very wrong of me to joke about people who can't read or rite. Oops. I mean* write. *Sorry again. I shall go and sit in the Naughty Corner for ten minutes.*

He dug his knees into Nobby's panting sides, and the tiny horse staggered forward.

Bogbrush turned in the saddle, almost knocking Nobby over. "I go first unto the Temple of the Great Belch, God of Barbarity. I must announce my quest and seek the blessings of Belch."

But by that time it was snowing again, and everyone had gone inside.

"I'll miss him a bit. He was our only son," said his mother as she poured a flagon of hot cider brewed from turnips.

"No he wasn't," replied his father. "We've got five other lads. They've just been hiding from Bogbrush."

"Oh, yes," said Bogbrush's mother. "I'd forgotten about them."

CHAPTER 4

(That's all my fingers except the pinky.)

Four, or perhaps nine, or six, days later, a huge figure on a tiny pony approached a massive rock. An entrance — like a cave but neater, as if someone with a ruler and pencil had drawn it — gaped in the sheer stone wall. Above the entrance was a series of carved symbols. Bogbrush knew that they were called runes. Runes of power. Grandfather Bumrash had told him about runes (which are really just scratchings, but *waaayyyy cooler*) and about the famous Temple of the Great Belch, where he himself had journeyed to get his barbarian license many, many moons before.

The symbols meant something important, like "Begone, strangers" or "Beware of dog." Or possibly "Happy Birthday, Sandra!" Bogbrush didn't know which, of course.

TODAY'S REVIEW: Remember when we discussed reading and writing, and how Bogbrush couldn't? Previous chapter. You were there. (Author makes smacking-head gesture.)

He spurred Nobby forward. Actually, he didn't use spurs because that would have been cruel. As it was, the little horse lurched forward and fell in front of the cave. Bogbrush took this as a sign from the God of Barbarity that he was at the right place.

"Right," he said. "Ho! You remain here, bold steed, ere I hath need of your speed and courage." Bogbrush knew that he ought to speak *even more* like a barbarian hero than usual. After all, he was at the Temple of the Great Belch, which was like the Barbarian Hall of Fame. Cave of Fame, really.

Nobby was quite willing to remain where he was. He stretched out, panting, eyes rolling. Bogbrush took his sword, axe and spear. Being a kindly soul, he gave the pony a big gulp of ale and a turnip sandwich. A hero must look after his horse. It's a rule.

Bogbrush strode toward the doorway, Headlopper in one hand and Nosebiter in the other. He'd thought of carrying Gutjabber in his teeth, but that would be awkward if anyone expected him to speak. Besides, the entrance might not be wide enough to pass through with a ruddy big spear in his mouth. He jabbed it into the ground, wishing he could tie a label with his name and address around the wooden shaft. That way nobody would steal it. Not if they were honest and literate, anyway.

Bogbrush was about to enter the Temple of the Great Belch, and he did not want anything embarrassing to happen on the way in. Someone might be watching.

Someone was. As Bogbrush stepped across the threshold, a deep voice boomed out, "Who dares enter the sanctuary of the Great Belch? The Temple of the God of Barbarity?"

Bogbrush pulled himself up to his full height. This would have looked grand if he hadn't banged his head on the top of the entrance, jamming his helmet down over his forehead. He was, as we've said, a very big fellow. "Ho! 'Tis I, Bogbrush, a mighty barbarian warrior from the far north. I come to — to —"

Bogbrush had to think for a minute about what he had come to do. It didn't help that he had banged his head and had a helmet rim over his eyes. There was a phrase that you had to say. He remembered it. "To pay my devotions to the Great Belch and announce my mighty quest."

"Same as all the other silly beggars," said the voice, although more quietly and from close by. Bogbrush peered into the Stygian gloom. A tiny figure, grinning, approached. "Morning, Bogbrush! Come in. Careful where you step — the Hellish Hounds have been in here, and I've not had time to mop."

PHRASE OF THE DAY: Stygian gloom — *pronounced "Stidge-ee-an." Very dark. As in "The room was filled with Stygian gloom until Uncle Bert found the spare lightbulbs, which were under the sink."*

The man was the size of a nine-year-old child, but wizened with age. He looked like a bald chimpanzee with a broom. "My name's Arfa," he said. "Janitor and general helper to the Great Belch. Just follow the hallway and knock at the door. The high priestess will look after you."

Bogbrush walked
carefully down a
long passageway lit
by flaming torches set
into the rock walls.
Ahead lay a great wooden
door with a brass knocker
the size of a chariot
wheel. Bogbrush listened.
There was a strange, high-
pitched wailing be-
yond the doorway.
He knocked. The
wailing ceased. He
wondered what sort of
fiendish creature could
make such a noise. Then
a woman's voice
called out.

"You caught me at
my daily wailing. I try to get in half an hour of
shrieking practice in the morning and half an hour
of groaning rehearsal before supper. Come on in,
dearie! It's not locked."

Bogbrush pushed open the door.

CHAPTER 5

(And there's the pinky!)

The great door creaked open slowly. There was a dim, flickery light, with deep shadow beneath. Bogbrush put one foot forward to step inside. As he did, his foot kicked a tiny stone. The pebble dropped into the darkness, rattling as it bounced off the sides of a deep chasm. The mighty barbarian peered downward and saw — with horror — that one more step would have plunged him to his doom. The door opened onto a sheer drop of — *whoops!* He grabbed the doorknob and dangled. How far was the floor below?

Bogbrush had no way of measuring. He guessed it was about as far as all the men in his village, standing on each other's shoulders, which they never did, because they didn't like each other that much.

INCREASE YOUR VOCABULARY: All these useful words suggest sheer drops onto hard floors a long way below: chasm, precipice, ravine, cliff, crevasse, oops, splat. Impress your teacher by using any of these in class.

Bogbrush was hanging over the precipice, clutching the handle as the massive door swung to and fro. His legs were pedaling madly in thin air. As the door came back, he reached out with his toes and found solid rock beneath his feet. He let go and landed upon the tiniest of ledges.

"Not bad," said a woman's voice. "Most of the new boys go over the Cliff of No Return. Or Cliff of Doom. We haven't decided which name to call it yet."

"Either one soundeth good," replied Bogbrush, happy to no longer dangle over the chasm. Or crevasse, whichever. "Who art thou? And how doth I get down?"

He heard two hands clap, and the lights burst on brightly. The woman's voice rang out, "Ladder on your left, dearie! No, the other left. Climb down and let's have a look at you."

Bogbrush climbed down to a stone bridge across the ravine. On the other side stood a beautiful woman in gossamer robes.

Actually, she looked like someone's grandmother in gossamer robes. Bogbrush did not realize this, because in his country grandmothers were all toothless and wrinkled and stirred cauldrons all day. It was a rule.

Bogbrush knew she had to be the high priestess of the temple. His grandfather had spoken of her as a glamorous lady, elegant of figure and with all her own teeth. She was bejeweled and

WORD OF THE DAY:
gossamer — *delicate and shimmery. See if you can use it in conversation with friends without any of them hitting you.*

bedecked in finery. You could tell she was not dressed for fetching the groceries or cleaning the oven. She smiled at Bogbrush.

"Hello, sonny! You're a big lad, aren't you?"

Bogbrush thought that he was. "I am mighty thew'd," he agreed.

The priestess crossed the bridge and approached

him. She poked the muscles in his shoulder. "You can help me get the coal up the stairs, then," she said. "My arthritis is acting up again."

"I wilt do any bold deed," declared Bogbrush, although he thought carrying sacks of coal up three flights of steps was not as heroic as, say, slaying dragons.

"I suppose you want to be a properly licensed barbarian hero with the official approval of the Great Belch. And you'll want the amulet of the Great Belch — yours for a low, low price today only."

Bogbrush wanted all that. "I do! What must I doeth to gain these bounteous gifts of the god?" he asked. As he looked at her closely he noticed that the priestess wore a thick layer of paint on her face, possibly plastered on with a trowel. He realized she might be older than she appeared. A lot older. Forty, or ninety, or something like that.

"There are three tests," said the high priestess. She'd put on a more impressive voice now. "Thou hast passed the first one by not tumbling off the Cliff of No Return, or Cliff of Doom, depending on which name we decide on. We're running a contest to pick a name. Free to enter! Fabulous prizes!"

"What lyeth at the foot of yon chasm beneath the cliff of which thou speakest?" asked Bogbrush, changing the subject. He wasn't really interested in what they *called* the chasm, cliff, ravine or precipice as long as he didn't fall over it himself.

"Skellingtons, mostly," replied the high priestess, losing her impressive voice again. "The bones of the silly devils who came here before you. We like to think of them as sacrificial victims."

Bogbrush had no idea what she meant by "sacrificial victims." Clearly his confusion (and failure to pay attention in class, hint, hint) showed on his face because the high priestess explained all about sacrificial victims.

"You know, persons as is throwed to their deaths to make the god happy. I don't know why, but gods are supposed to like that sort of thing — at least, this one does. We used to ask for beautiful maidens to volunteer for it, but they always said they were washing their hair instead. So we just go with the clumsy barbarians wot falls in. I think the Great Belch is all right with that, really."

CAREER TIPS: If your school counselor suggests that "sacrificial victim" is the sort of job you might qualify for, you can assume he or she does not think your skills and talents are impressive. Take some summer school classes or go to night school. At least try to pull your grades up to a D. Let some other sucker with crummy grades be the sacrificial victim!

Bogbrush didn't know what to think. It wasn't what he was good at. But he didn't have to think anymore because the high priestess continued, "Next task is to fight the monstrous servant of the Great Belch. You'll enjoy that."

CHAPTER 6

(I'm holding up another finger now.)

Fighting monsters was exactly the sort of thing Bogbrush was good at. He'd spent a lot of time practicing, as we know. So when a huge, brutish-looking figure shambled out of a tunnel behind the high priestess, the warrior knew what to do. He drew Headlopper, and with one mighty blow struck the vile creature's head clean off its shoulders.

A gush of foul blood sprayed across the chamber as the monster fell in a heap. Quite a lot of it went on the priestess's dress. She didn't look pleased.

"Sorry about that," said Bogbrush.

"Dry cleaning bills will kill me," muttered the high priestess. "And talking of killing, that bloke you chopped up wasn't *actually* the monstrous servant you've got to fight. That was Harold, who does the dirty dishes. *Did* the dirty dishes, I should say. He was going to take you to meet the monstrous servant."

"Er, sorry, again," said Bogbrush. One day he would slay a monster. So far he'd slain three cows, two pigs and a dishwasher.

The high priestess smiled. "Never mind. I never much liked Harold. Bad breath and sloppy work with the pan scrubber. Just go on down the hallway until you hear the screaming. The monstrous servant will be there."

Bogbrush walked into the tunnel, stepping around the blood, since he only had the one pair of boots.

As the high priestess had told him, the lair of the monstrous servant was easily found. It was the cave with the screaming. It wasn't the cave that was screaming, of course. Somebody inside was having a bad day.

Bogbrush tapped on the door and called out. "Anybody home?"

A voice yelled something that might have been

"Help me! I'm being gobbled alive by a humongous man-eating demon!"

But to Bogbrush, it sounded more like "Eeeyaaah! Owwwww! Aaaggh!" So he tapped again.

The screaming stopped, and Bogbrush took this as a sign that he should go in now. His mother had always tried to teach him to be polite.

GOOD MANNERS: Remember always to knock before entering, and don't go in until you've been told to come in, or the screaming ceases.

Bogbrush was in a vast chamber that seemed to go back as far as the Chasm of Death (or whatever). It was littered with bones and rusted armor. In the center stood a creature so huge, so hideous, so disgusting that Bogbrush had no words to describe him. In fact, I don't have words to describe him, and I'm the one making him up. You could tell he was a servant from the neat white apron he wore, which he was using to wipe the blood from his jagged fangs.

"Be'st thou the fabled monstrous servant?" asked Bogbrush.

The monster stood on his hind legs, looking down at our hero with red eyes glowing like those horrible candies that burn your throat when you suck on them. He had the last few inches of a pair of feet sticking out of his mouth. A few moments of chewing, and even the toes were gone. The creature burped and licked his lips with a tongue like a pound of raw liver.

He spoke politely. It was a horrible, rasping voice, but very well mannered. "Good morning, sir. A barbarian gentleman? Crunchy on the outside, soft center within. Yummy. I'll attend to you now, sir. Which means I'll eat you."

Bogbrush stepped forward into the chamber. The monster was gargantuan, the size of a house. Twice the size of the houses in Bogbrush's village, which were small and built without scenic views, attractive amenities and modern conveniences. It was "a ruddy great flipping walloping thing," as his grandfather would have said. Bumrash had a poetic streak to him.

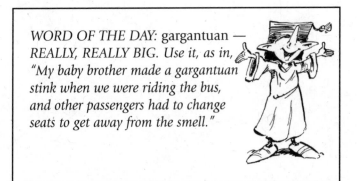

WORD OF THE DAY: gargantuan — *REALLY, REALLY BIG. Use it, as in, "My baby brother made a gargantuan stink when we were riding the bus, and other passengers had to change seats to get away from the smell."*

The monstrous servant flicked a toothpick the size of a spear through the air, missing Bogbrush by inches.

The toothpick struck the wall and splintered.

The barbarian hero weighed his weapons in either hand. His face bore a look of ferocious ferocity, which was very ferocious indeed.

"Prepare to meet thy doom," said Bogbrush.

CHAPTER 7

(Uh-huh, one whole hand and these two fingers.)

The monstrous servant laughed. It was a booming, sinister sort of laugh that echoed through the cavern. Most people would have been terrified. Bogbrush simply gripped Headlopper and Nosebiter more tightly. He didn't like being laughed at.

"I shall cleave thee in twain. Or more bits than that!" declared the barbarian.

The monster laughed again. "As you wish, sir!"

Then a mighty fist slammed down mere inches from Bogbrush, and he jumped to one side. Many people might say "he jumped in fright," but I won't. It was a *tactical move* on his part. A second fist slammed down on the other side, and Bogbrush made another tactical move, backward, on his chain mail–clad buttocks. Chafing was involved.

The fist was as big as a cart horse.

Bogbrush began to think that perhaps this wasn't going to be as easy as he'd expected.

"I give thee one chance to surrender with honor!" he shouted. Perhaps the monstrous servant would simply give in when he understood he was facing a mighty hero, a dauntless (remember that word?) warrior.

Or maybe not.

"Most considerate of you, sir," replied the monster. Another blow came and whapped Bogbrush across the cavern. He dropped his axe. His helmet toppled off. The pouch on his belt opened, its contents tumbling out. Four copper coins, a broken comb and a turnip sandwich.

Bogbrush flung himself across the floor as a second blow crushed his helmet flat. He grabbed the axe and rolled over as a mighty kick (from a foot larger than a pigsty) missed his barbarian bottom.

Then there was a moment of stillness.

"I say, sir. Is that a turnip sandwich I see before me?"

Bogbrush looked down. It was indeed a turnip sandwich. A large, perfectly formed turnip sandwich, with delectable slivers of root vegetable delicately placed between slices of grayish chewy bread. His mother's finest work and a special favorite at home — much better than the turnip porridge, turnip cake or turnip pie that she also served for supper. They grew a lot of turnips.

"I really like turnip sandwiches," said the monstrous servant. "When I've killed you and chewed your legs off — I prefer to dine headfirst — I shall finish the meal with that delicious-looking turnip sandwich. And a cup of decaf."

Bogbrush didn't like the sound of that. Mostly the first part of it; he didn't care much about the sandwich, or what sort of coffee the monster drank. What did he care if the huge man-eating creature became jumpy and irritable after too much caffeine? He had other things to worry about.

KNOW YOUR ROOT VEGETABLES: The turnip (brassica rapa) *is a plant of the mustard family, common in northern climes, bearing a fleshy edible root of whitish color. Ask your mother to make you a turnip sandwich or other tasty turnip-based snacks. If you own an ice-cream maker, you are in for a special treat!*

Still, a barbarian hero must be heroic. If he dies, he dies heroically. And if he was going to die heroically by being stomped underfoot and chomped down like a cookie, he'd at least defy his slayer by one small gesture.

"I defy thee with this gesture!" shouted Bogbrush as he seized the turnip sandwich. "This, at least, I shalt deny thee."

And he denied the monstrous servant by throwing the turnip sandwich into the chasm. Over the Cliff of Whatever. A gentle underarm toss, such as you might use in a game of catch with a heavily medicated senior citizen with poor eyesight and only one arm.

Don't laugh. Some people aren't as lucky as you are.

"Noooooooooooohhhhh!" yelled the monster. "Noooooooooooohhhhhhoooooooohhhh! Not the turnip sandwich!"

With a mighty leap, the monstrous servant dived for the falling sandwich, and disappeared over the edge of the precipice. The word "Noooooooooohhhhhhoooohhhh!!!" echoed and faded away.

GEOGRAPHICAL NOTE: *Some of you may be asking, "Why is the Cliff of ~~Whatever~~ (ENTER THE "NAME THIS CHASM" CONTEST!) in the same cave as the monstrous servant, when clearly Bogbrush had to walk down a hallway away from the very same Cliff of Thingummy about ten pages ago?" I'll let you into a secret. This is a fantasy book. In fantasy books there are no actual floor plans. If there were, there'd be laundry rooms, fire exits, bathrooms and attics filled with stacks of old National Geographic magazines. But there aren't. Nobody ever uses the toilet in a fantasy book. Well, most fantasy books. So quit whining about where the %$#* cliff is or isn't, smart aleck —*

CHAPTER 8

(That's quite a lot, isn't it? I had no idea I had so many fingers.)

Bogbrush stood and peered over the edge of the cliff. It was jet black down there. Stygian gloom. (Remember that one?)

"Thou hast met thy just deserts!" he declared.

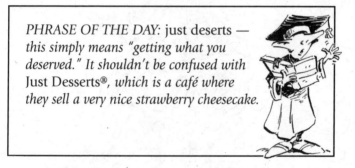

*PHRASE OF THE DAY: just deserts —
this simply means "getting what you
deserved." It shouldn't be confused with*
Just Desserts®, *which is a café where
they sell a very nice strawberry cheesecake.*

The mighty warrior congratulated himself on the success of his plan. His brilliant scheme. His bold strategy. Within a minute he had persuaded himself that the whole thing had been exactly what he'd intended all along. The *turnip sandwich trick.* Clever. Very clever.

Bogbush picked up his crushed helmet and was just about to stride manfully back to find the high priestess when a voice boomed from deep below, "I'll be back to finish you off, sir, just as soon as I finish this excellent sandwich!"

Bogbrush decided it was time to go. *Now.*

He returned down the hallway to the great chamber. "'Tis I, Bogbrush, vanquisher of evil," he announced.

The high priestess was painting her toenails a vivid shade of purple. She seemed astonished to see the young hero alive and undamaged. "Oh … Bogbrush," she stammered. "Yes, of course. I was, ah, expecting you. Did you defeat the monstrous servant? Did you kill him?"

"I did lay him low in battle, aye," said Bogbrush. "But I spared his life, for he was a valiant foe."

"Oh, that's a relief," said the priestess. "You'd be amazed how hard it is to get good help." Then she flashed her wondrous priestessy smile. Bogbrush jumped back from the glare of her shiny white, perfectly formed teeth; he wasn't used to old ladies having any teeth at all.

"Now you have passed the second test," she intoned. "Few doth get this far. Most gets ate — er, eaten before now. You really are a mighty one, aren't you, dearie? Just right to help me move this altar. It's too heavy for me to lift. I think my nail clippers might have fallen underneath it." The high priestess pointed to a splendid, obviously ancient altar. It was a vast slab of marble standing on stone pedestals. Carved on its surface was the image of the great god Belch. Anyone could tell it was a sacred object of great age and holiness. Well, anyone except Bogbrush, who simply shoved the altar aside, denting it and scratching the floor. Beneath lay the missing nail clippers, together with an emery board, a copy of *TV GUIDE* for the week before last Christmas and enough dust bunnies to stock a pet shop.

The priestess clapped her hands. "Ooh! You passed another test, dearie!" She grinned and pinched Bogbrush on his mighty barbarian cheek. Reaching past him to a curtained alcove, she brought out a small golden cage. Something chattered inside it.

"And now the very last test," she said. "The test wot makes mighty warriors quail and faint away in terror."

"I fear naught," announced Bogbrush in his best heroic voice.

"Yeah, well, they all say that," muttered the priestess. "Until they sees it." She turned toward Bogbrush and held up the cage. Inside, tiny black eyes stared balefully at the barbarian. Fierce whiskers and savage teeth were mere inches from his face. It had terrifying ears, as well. Bogbrush blinked at the fiendish creature. He'd seen nothing like it before.

"Behold!" said the High Priestess in her most commanding voice. "Behold the Gerbil of Fate."

CHAPTER 9

**(This would be both hands raised
if I had lost a finger like Uncle Bob who
had that unfortunate accident
with the bacon slicer.)**

Bogbrush somehow knew he shouldn't laugh. A little voice inside his head said, Don't laugh. No chuckling. Hold the giggles. Guffaw not.

This was lucky for Bogbrush, really, because the high priestess looked into his eyes. "Yes, dearie, I'm glad you take it seriously. Lots of boys don't and, well, it upsets the gerbil."

"What happeneth when the gerbil is upset?" he asked.

A frown darkened the priestess's beautiful (although heavily painted) face. "Things. Nasty things. I'll tell you when we begin the test."

Bogbrush listened as she explained the test, and he understood why grown men feared and bold men fainted. "I put him on top of your head," said the priestess. "And he sits there for hours and contemplates your destiny in a mysterious fashion. He examines your heroic prospects. That's all."

Bogbrush wasn't at all sure he wanted the Gerbil of Fate to examine his heroic prospects. It could leave off contemplating his destiny as well. He was just glad he hadn't laughed at the gerbil. The gerbil might want to get the last laugh. Still …

"I am ready for the test," he announced. He removed his helmet.

The priestess placed the gerbil on Bogbrush's head. The young barbarian stood stock-still. He felt a warm moistness leak over his scalp but kept silent.

After a few minutes the priestess said, "Let me know if he tinkles on your head."

Bogbrush looked at her. "He hath done so already, sometime past."

The high priestess burst out laughing. "All right, duckie, you pass." She reached up and gently picked up the gerbil, holding it so that its rodenty behind did not come into contact with her hand.

"I passeth?" asked Bogbrush.

"That's all nonsense I just told you. It's only a pet gerbil. His name's Binky. I always tell that story to see if my heroes in the making can face their fears. A lot of big strapping warriors get very nervous, I can tell you. A little pet animal widdles on their head and they get all … bothered."

Bogbrush smiled the special smile of the truly stupid.

The Gerbil of Fate chewed on a nut and blinked at Bogbrush.

"Congratulations, sweetie. You're in! A fully certified barbarian hero, backed by all the power of the Great Belch! There's a very nice amulet that'll go with your eyes, and a list of our members all over the world. We think most of 'em are still alive. You can call on any licensed barbarian for help in hacking, slaying and plundering. Likewise, they can expect you to do your bit for them in times of need. Or want. Or just for a bit of barbaric company." She handed over a medallion the size of a cabbage on a golden chain. Bogbrush thought it looked better than a cabbage. It was yellow and shiny and had carvings on it.

WORD OF THE DAY: amulet — *a token of good fortune, or even magic. Much better than a rabbit's foot or a lucky penny. Some amulets ward off evil, like "protection from homework."*

The priestess also handed him a purse full of gold coins, which are always useful, and a very handsome certificate in its own plastic frame.

"I thank thee," said Bogbrush. "I shall venture toward the lands of the south."

"Fun in the sun," she replied. "Very nice for you, duckie! Be careful about sunburn. You'll regret it when you are my age. I have to work hard to cover the wrinkles — I mean, to maintain my timeless beauty. You could stay here, if you like. Them sacks of coal aren't moving themselves."

"Alas," answered Bogbrush, "I must mount my steed and go forth."

"On a quest, then?"

"Aye," agreed Bogbrush. "I questeth questfully."

The high priestess looked at him eye to eye.

Since he was two heads taller than she was, she had to stand on a chair to do this. "You've got no flippin' idea what this quest is, do you, dear?"

Bogbrush hung his head. He had no flippin' idea what his quest was all about. His plan was simply to ride around on Nobby's back, slaying things as usual. Other people's cows and pigs, mostly. It was the best scheme he could think of.

The priestess went on. "I must tell thee the tale of the Axe in the Stone, which is like the much more famous Sword in the Stone, but *very slightly* different, what with it being an axe and all that. In the city of Scrofula a great axe is embedded in a humongous rock and, according to legend, the axe can only be pulled out by the True King of Scrofula."

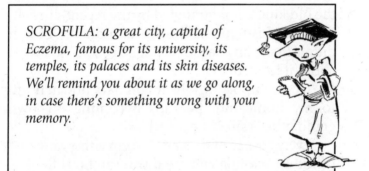

SCROFULA: a great city, capital of Eczema, famous for its university, its temples, its palaces and its skin diseases. We'll remind you about it as we go along, in case there's something wrong with your memory.

"Is there no king in Scrofula, then?" Bogbrush asked.

"Not in years and years, dearie. There's a bloke wot's called a 'regent' in charge. The one there now is the son of the last one, who was the son of the one before that," replied the priestess.

"What happenedeth to the last True King?"

"The story is that he went out alone on horseback one day, leaving his axe thrust into the rock for when he returned," explained the priestess. "Only he never came back."

"I'd have put it in a closet," said Bogbrush, "so that nobody tripped over it."

"Yeah," agreed the priestess. "Or on a nice presentation rack over the fireplace. But anyway, that's the legend. The True King, who is the son of the son of the son of the last king, whoever he might be, will return and claim his throne again." The priestess muttered something under her breath that the barbarian didn't understand. Something about the old king being strangled by the regent's henchmen and his remains thrown in a ditch. But that didn't make any sense to Bogbrush, so he forgot about it immediately.

"Do you think the king might have ridden north to my homeland, perhaps becoming my own grandfather's sire?" he asked.

"Every chance of it, dearie. Worth a shot, anyway! Go on to Scrofula and see if you can hoist the axe. The first regent built a very nice temple around the rock — it's called the Shrine of the Axe — and every year there's a ceremony where lucky contestants try to tug out the axe. Nobody's managed it yet." She put on her impressive, I'm-SOOO-important voice again. "Mount thy mighty steed, O Bogbrush, and follow thy destiny. Also, watch thy step and mind thy head."

Bogbrush was so filled with barbaric joy at the thought of following his destiny that he took no notice of the priestess's other advice. He tripped on the steps and banged his head on the top of the doorway, jamming his helmet down over his eyes. As he staggered blindly from the temple in search of the noble Nobby, Bogbrush heard the high priestess bid him farewell.

"Toodle-ooh, duckie. Come back anytime. You can help me move the furniture again!"

IMPORTANT NOTE: Some of you may be nervous about the Gerbil of Fate. Rest assured that this animal is a fictional character and will not examine your heroic prospects in any way. Sleep tight.

CHAPTER 10
(That IS both hands raised!)

Bogbrush rode south. Southish, really. Arfa had pointed out the direction, and given him a big bag of food for the journey. Three (or eight) days from the Temple of the Great Belch, across desert plains, rugged purple hills and a few flower patches — which Nobby ate — the pair came to a village. It wasn't much of a village, but Bogbrush had nothing to compare it to except his own.

"Ho, Nobby, what a fine city!" he exclaimed. "I believe a hundred people must live here. Or maybe a million. The huts are made of a special kind of mud!"

The barbarian had never seen buildings made from bricks before.

"And they have special places by the sides of the pathway, where all the dung and dead rats and chicken bones lyeth. What marvels!"

Bogbrush had never seen gutters before either.

In his village, if you had a bucket of dung or a bag of dead rats, you just threw them anywhere. "This, Nobby, is civilization."

WORD OF THE DAY: civilization — *a place where there are special spots to throw dung and dead rats.*

A man with one eye, one leg and one arm was sweeping the step of one of the wondrous brick buildings. He nodded at Bogbrush.

"You look like a man who could use a drink," he said.

"You looketh like a man who couldst use extra body parts," replied Bogbrush. "Yet I shalt drink, as wilt my steed."

The man smiled. He'd lost most of his teeth, as well. "Welcome to Lucky's, the best tavern in Upper Malaria. Bad ale, crummy food, terrible service. Nicest place in a hundred leagues in any direction."

"How far be'eth a league?" asked Bogbrush. If it was, say, about the distance between his ear and his elbow, he'd push on to a nicer place.

"Too far, traveler," replied the tavern keeper. "Come in. I'm Lucky. It's my place."

"Why do they call thee Lucky?" asked Bogbrush.

"I had a brother who never seemed to get any of the good fortune that has come my way," replied Lucky. "We call him the Dear Departed, or the Late Lamented. Or Squashy."

Bogbrush walked into a low, dark room. Actually, he walked into the top of the doorway — "OOF!" — then ducked and went into the low, dark room. Music was playing, and a woman in shadow sang a mournful melody of love titled "Get off My Foot, You Oaf."

"I wilt have a flagon of thy finest ale," said Bogbrush.

"It's all 'orrible," replied an old man in the corner.

"Vile stuff," said his drinking partner.

"Disgusting," said a third voice. This was Lucky himself.

"I'll have that, then," said Bogbrush. "Let me put my things down." He put his axe down by heaving it toward a corner of the room.

"Be careful with that valuable antique chair!" shouted Lucky. But it was hard to hear him over the sound of splintering furniture.

"Sorry!" Bogbrush apologized. "Still, it was pretty old, was it not?"

He put his spear away by impaling an oil painting on the wall.

CHAPTER 11

(I have to take my right shoe off now.)

There were a number of people seated at long tables. Bogbrush, of course, didn't know what that number was. The music had changed to a delicate instrumental version of a traditional ballad, "There's a Mammoth Stuck under My Bed, Grandma."

"You, sir!" called out a man with gold teeth and a wide smile. "Would you wish to engage in a game of chance? Perhaps a small wager? Just in fun?"

Gambling. Bogbrush's mother had always warned him against gambling. But that was before he was a fully licensed barbarian hero.

"Why not?" said Bogbrush as he sat down.

"Because he'll rob you blind," said a quiet voice. Bogbrush couldn't hear the words over the music.

The man stretched out a hand. "I am Lucidar. A poor traveler. I simply play for the joy of the game."

"Joy of taking your money," said the quiet voice. Bogbrush still couldn't quite hear it.

Lucidar was a thin man with greasy black hair and a pointy beard. He wore purple robes with wide sleeves, like a magician or a library assistant. He was riffling through a deck of cards. He cut the deck, shuffled them at lightning speed and did an amazing trick in which all the cards leaped from one hand

into the other in exact sequence. Bogbrush thought
that Lucidar might have played before.

"Pick a card!" said Lucidar.

Bogbrush did so. His card had tiny pictures, all
the same, of an axe.

"It's got tiny pictures of —"

"Shhh!" whispered Lucidar very loudly. "Do not
tell me what cards thou doth have!"

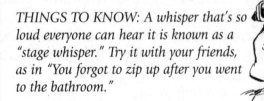

THINGS TO KNOW: *A whisper that's so
loud everyone can hear it is known as a
"stage whisper." Try it with your friends,
as in "You forgot to zip up after you went
to the bathroom."*

"I shall guess the card," Lucidar continued. "Hold the card to your chest, my friend. What suit, then. Swords? Mice? Axes? Chickens? A king or a priest or a lowly three?"

WORD OF THE DAY: suit — *a group of cards with the same markings. Hearts, diamonds, spades and socks, for instance, are the suits you are probably familiar with.*

Bogbrush held the card tight.

"It's the four of mice!" announced Lucidar.

Bogbrush showed the card. People at the table gasped. "No, wrong, it's the nine of axes!"

"Ah," said Lucidar, slapping his forehead. "I have so little skill! Yet, would ye play with me, barbaric friend? For the sport of it?"

Bogbrush thought that perhaps Lucidar wasn't very good, after all. Why not play a hand of these "cards"?

"Here is a simple game, such as I know how to play," said Lucidar. "I deal thee five cards. Thou puts money on the table. Then I deal ten cards for me. If your cards add up to more than mine, I give thee coins of the same amount as thou have bet. If not, I take thy money."

"All right," said Bogbrush.

"He's cheating you," said that same quiet voice.

Bogbrush heard it this time. But he didn't know what the voice was talking about. How could his new friend be cheating him? Why, Lucidar was simply showing him how to play the game!

Lucidar dealt him five cards. Two of the cards had pictures of tiny swords, lots of them. One had a big picture of a chicken wearing a crown. The rest had little pictures of mice, one with just a few, the other with many. Exactly how many was a complete mystery to the barbarian.

"Place your bet," announced Lucidar. Bogbrush reached into his pouch and laid out three copper coins. Lucidar looked at the coins — enough to buy a stale turnip sandwich and a cup of dirty water — and dealt himself ten cards. He flipped them over. They were all ones, twos and threes of the different suits.

"Oh, what bad luck!" said Lucidar. "My own cards add up to twenty-five. Yours add up to twenty-six. You must be better than I am! Here's three copper pieces." He gave Bogbrush a sly look. "If you'll let me try again, we might use some of those gold coins I see in your pouch. They are much prettier than the ugly copper ones."

Bogbrush jingled some coins in his hand, and agreed that the golden ones that the high priestess had given him were a lot nicer than the thin copper pieces. They were heavier and shinier, and had pictures of a man in a crown on them, like the chicken on the card he'd just played. That was a lucky sign!

The voice behind him made the same noise his mother had always made just before he was about to do something foolish. Bogbrush looked around, but his mother was nowhere to be seen. He brought out a handful of the gold coins …

CHAPTER 12

(And my right sock.)

Lucidar dealt another five cards. Bogbrush noticed that a big crowd had gathered around the table. The music ceased. He noticed that the singer had come over and was peering at Lucidar with the sort of look his mother always wore whenever her mighty barbarian son picked up the cows by their horns.

Bogbrush also noticed that this new hand of cards had very few of those pretty little pictures on them. He'd really liked those pictures.

A small, gray man came out of the gents' lavatory and sat on the bench next to him. Bogbrush wrinkled his brow at the cards.

"They all add up to nine, mate," said the gray man out of the corner of his mouth.

"Is that good?" asked Bogbrush.

"Not if 'ee's going to draw ten cards," replied the man. "Think about it."

In fact, Lucidar's ten cards added up to ninety-six. He reached for the pile of coins in front of Bogbrush.

It was hard to tell exactly what happened next. As Lucidar stretched forward, something struck him on the back. He jerked up in surprise and threw his arms out wide. Cards fell out of his sleeve. Dice fell out of his sleeve. Half a roast chicken fell out of his sleeve.

"Cheat!" shouted one onlooker. "Cardsharp!" yelled another. "That's my lunch!" called a third. The singer was inspecting her nails and whistling, acting as if it had nothing to do with her.

Bogbrush realized, at last, that the voice had been right. "This varlet hath cheated me!" he yelled. "I shall wreak vengeance on his head." He reached for his sword. It was gone. He looked for his axe. It wasn't there. He put his hand on his pouch. Nuh-uh. The gold coins on the table were missing. His helmet had disappeared from his head. His spear no longer jutted from the wall.

He turned to the little gray man beside him. The little gray man had gone as well.

Bogbrush picked up the table and broke it over Lucidar's head. The cardsharp went down in a heap of splinters. Bogbrush dropped a heavy wooden bench on him, just because. He stepped on Lucidar's ear, simply for the fun of it. But that was enough because he'd lost interest in the cheating gambler. What the barbarian hero wanted was to get his belongings back.

Bogbrush invoked his god. "Mighty Belch, Lord of Barbarity, help me regaineth my, uh, stuff!" he called out. His hand went to the sacred amulet of the Great Belch, hanging from a gold chain around his neck. Last seen hanging from a gold chain around his neck.

WORD OF THE DAY: invoke — *to call upon a god, as in, "O great God of Homework, make that which I did on the bus this morning suffice for a passing grade!"*

A man seated near the window had something important to tell Bogbrush.

"I think he's running away on your horse!"

CHAPTER 13
(You should know to stand back when I take my socks off.)

Bogbrush burst into action. He hurled himself through the window, taking most of the wall with him. There would have been shattered glass everywhere, if it had been invented yet.

"Oi!" shouted the landlord, Lucky. "You'll pay for the damage!"

Bogbrush wasn't listening. Nobody was going to steal his horse. He ran for the hitching post, where the tiny pony was rearing up to fight the man dressed in gray. The thief was trying desperately to untie the reins. Nobby was small but fierce, kicking and biting. The man was weighed down by a bundle of things he'd wrapped in his cloak. Big, hefty things. Before Bogbrush had a chance to grab the thief, Nobby swiped the fellow with a mighty blow of his front hooves. The thief went down like a sack of turnips. The cloak spilled open, and Bogbrush could see what fell out.

The sword Headlopper. The axe known as Nosebiter. A spear with a slightly ripped oil painting stuck on the spiky end. A helmet, slightly crushed. A pouch. Gold coins. Chain-mail underwear. Bogbrush hadn't noticed *that* was missing. This man was good at his work.

The mighty barbarian seized the thief and held him upside down in one huge hand. He poked the helpless man with his forefinger, so that the fellow swung back and forth with every pointy jab. Money, rings, necklaces and bracelets fell with every swing. The gray man's clothes were full of secret pockets.

"Why!" *Swing!* "Why didst thou steal my possessions?" shouted Bogbrush. The man was sick from being swung about. His face was as gray as his clothing.

"It's what I do, guv'nor. I steal things. It's my job. No offense meant," he spluttered.

WORD OF THE DAY: guv'nor
— *short for "governor." Slang for "boss" or "chief." Your mother might enjoy being called* guv'nor. *Or she might not.*

"You are a thief!" announced Bogbrush.

"Of course I am," replied the man. "Do you think I do this for fun? Running about with big blokes chasing me, and getting kicked by 'orses? It's an 'ard job, it is. Put me down, if you don't mind. I've got to pee again."

A crowd had gathered in the street. Lucky, the tavern keeper, was yelling at Bogbrush for damaging his inn, and at the gray man for stealing inside his tavern. Most of all he was screaming at the singer, who was arguing back.

"Look at that," said the gray man. "Lucky is such a scoundrel! A proper 'ippo-crit.

ANOTHER WORD OF THE DAY: 'ippo-crit — *actually* hypocrite, *pronounced more or less as the thief says it, but with an* h *on the front. It means somebody who says one thing and does another. When you take six cookies and your brother takes three, tell him how greedy he is. That's what I'm talking about!*

He lets me pick pockets in 'is tavern as long as I gives 'im a share. He lets that crooked card dealer rob the customers — taking a share for himself, of course."

"And now 'ee's shouting at Diphtheria," continued the gray man. "Just 'cos she don't like no dishonest dealings. Very fair is Diphtheria."

Bogbrush stared at the young woman called Diphtheria. She was tall and slender, and very fair indeed. Her hair was long and blond. Her skin was gleaming and brown. Her eyes were sparkling and green. Her clothes were ... interesting. She wore a shiny dress that might have been made of real silver, Bogbrush thought. It was pretty tight, but that was probably because silver was expensive, he reasoned. There was a gap in the middle, which revealed a massive red ruby in her belly button. (Bogbrush thought the gap must have saved her even more money.) She had bangles on her arms and legs, and sandals on her feet. It wasn't a costume you'd wear to feed the pigs.

The young warrior had never seen an outfit like it. Nobody dressed that way in his village. Well, it would have been far too cold, for one thing.

"Nice girl, Diphtheria," the thief went on. Since Bogbrush was still holding him upside down in mid-air, the fellow was addressing the barbarian's oversized kneecaps. Bogbrush had at last stopped poking him, which he seemed to appreciate. "Big ambitions. She's a singer, an actress and a conjurer. Don't know what she's doing in a one-'orse town like this."

Nobby neighed. He was the one horse in this town.

Diphtheria stopped arguing with Lucky. She simply punched him in the head. *Ker-thwack!* He went down like an even bigger sack of turnips. *Ba-dump!* She wiped the dust from her hands and walked over to Bogbrush.

"Greetings, barbarian," she said in a quiet voice. "My name is Diphtheria. The person you are holding is known as Sneaky. I apologize for his robbing you, but it's his job. He has a license. 'Certified pickpocket.' Let him down, as he will certainly need to urinate. You don't want to be holding him up in front of you. Let's go back inside and take some refreshment. Lucky will pay for us."

Lucky was still groaning in the gutter. That's where the dead rats and dung were kept, as you'll remember.

CHAPTER 14

(See, that's two complete hands and a whole foot, I think.)

They were back inside the tavern. Diphtheria had shown them to an unbroken table while Sneaky visited the gents' room. On his return, Sneaky had helped himself to two flagons of the disgusting ale and a cup of wine for the lady.

"Me thievin' license," he said to Bogbrush as he spread out a sheet of parchment.

WORD OF THE DAY: parchment — *it's like paper but more medieval, brown and crinkly. Like your grandfather, really.*

The sheet was covered with what the barbarian knew to be something called "writing."

"It says 'ere I am allowed to steal, rob, pickpocket and pinch goods and money to the value of 500 copper coins every month. After that, I 'ave to stop until the first day o' the next month. If I goes over the 500, I 'ave to take some time off, or share it with a less skilled, successful thief. Or — accordin' to the rules — give it back to the owner."

"Huh?" said Bogbrush.

"He's quite right," said Diphtheria. "He's allowed to steal so much but not a penny more. There's an office where he has to take his thievings to be valued. I don't think he's ever given anything back, though."

She took a drink and pulled a face at the taste. "Horrid stuff. Anyway, here's my idea. We should get together and leave this nasty little village behind. You, Mr. Barbarian, have the muscles. I have the brains. Sneaky has — well, Sneaky has a lot of things. A tiny bladder, for one thing. And he's friends with all sorts of useful lowlifes."

"Why shouldst I need thy comradeship?" demanded Bogbrush. "I am mighty Bogbrush, fully licensed barbarian hero. I smite, I slay. I redden the grass with the blood of mine enemies. I go on a mighty quest to free the Axe in the Stone and prove that I am the one True King of Scrofula. Maybe."

"You're an idiot," said Sneaky. "No offense intended, but you are three buckets short of a cartload."

"Huh?" said Bogbrush.

"My point exactly," replied the thief. "You need 'elp. Take this Axe in the Stone nonsense, for a start. Every idiot with big muscles has tried to pull it out. They all fail. Everyone laughs at them, and they slope off back to where they came from, tails between their legs."

"Tails between their legs?" asked Bogbrush. "I hath none tails!"

Sneaky groaned to himself.

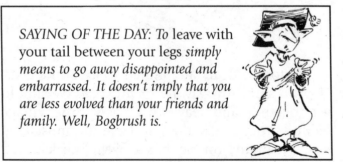

SAYING OF THE DAY: To leave with your tail between your legs *simply means to go away disappointed and embarrassed. It doesn't imply that you are less evolved than your friends and family. Well, Bogbrush is.*

Diphtheria leaned forward. "We should join a merchant caravan headed southward to Scrofula, if that's where you wish to go. You can get a job as a guard. I can sing for my living. And Sneaky's got his license. Caravans are always looking for a proper, certified thief. It keeps out the riffraff."

ANOTHER WORD OF THE DAY:
riffraff — *people so worthless that compared with them, Sneaky seems like a fine upstanding young man.*

Bogbrush suddenly realized where he'd heard Diphtheria's voice before. She'd been the one telling him that Lucidar was a cheat.

"Forsooth, 'tis a bold plan," declared Bogbrush. "Ho! For the scented cities of the south!"

"Wossee say?" asked Sneaky.

"Never mind," replied Diphtheria. "It'll only take me a moment to get my belongings."

"Yeah, and I 'ave to visit the little boys' room," announced Sneaky.

CHAPTER 15

(Okay, now THAT's two hands and a foot.)

Diphtheria was ready in two minutes, which was amazing when Bogbrush saw how many boxes, bags, barrels and trunks she had.

"I've got used to leaving places in a hurry," she explained. "Rough places."

"But what hast thou in thy baggage, fair maiden?" asked Bogbrush.

TRANSLATION: *"What's in the bags, toots?"*

"This contains my costumes," Diphtheria replied, picking up a bag. She pulled out a series of silken dresses, like a conjurer performing a magic trick. "This one contains my wigs." She pointed to a very large, round box. "This strange device here plays the music I sing to — you put a copper coin in and pick any tune you like. The barrel contains cheap jewelry, which shines nicely when I perform, but I don't care if anyone steals it. I get it by the bucket from Sneaky. The young thieves use it to practice on. Take a handful, if you want."

Bogbrush looked into the barrel of gleaming gold and jewels. "But — 'tis a king's ransom!" he declared.

"Only if you don't want to rescue the king. It's all fake, and comes in wagonloads from a factory in the farthest east — I believe it's made of sawdust, ground-up bones and paint. Anyone who steals it is an idiot," said Diphtheria.

Just then Sneaky appeared with a donkey and cart. "Transport, m'lady!" he announced. Bogbrush looked at the thief with a stern expression.

"Yet another theft, rogue?" he said.

"Just borrowed it from a friend," replied Sneaky. "It was parked outside the gents' room. I'll give it back, I swear."

"Oh, that's all right, then," replied Bogbrush.

Diphtheria laughed.

Bogbrush was good at lifting heavy things, like boxes and cows, so it took only a minute to get all the baggage in the cart. "What keepest thou in all these boxes?" he asked Diphtheria. "More jewels? More earwigs?"

"Wigs, not earwigs, silly!" she said, laughing. "Those contain my laboratory equipment. Vials, phials, burners, slides, samples, test tubes, that sort of thing. I study the science of alchemy."

Bogbrush had no idea what she was talking about.

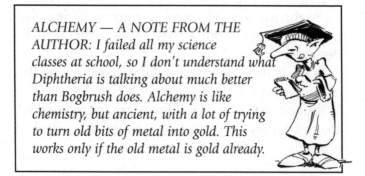

ALCHEMY — A NOTE FROM THE AUTHOR: I failed all my science classes at school, so I don't understand what Diphtheria is talking about much better than Bogbrush does. Alchemy is like chemistry, but ancient, with a lot of trying to turn old bits of metal into gold. This works only if the old metal is gold already.

"I plan on becoming a professional alchemist," she explained. "I applied to the university in Scrofula, but they won't let me attend. They have a sign that says NO GIRLS ALLOWED. Pigs!" She spat, but in a ladylike way.

Diphtheria smiled at Bogbrush. "You have no idea what I am talking about, do you?" she said. "Let me show you a trick. Give me your bag of gold."

Bogbrush handed over the purse he'd been given by the high priestess.

Diphtheria chanted an incantation while gesturing dramatically over the bag. Then there was a sudden flash of green smoke. Bogbrush was startled and jumped to his feet. Diphtheria grinned, pointing toward the purse. "Behold — I have turned your gold into lead!" Bogbrush examined the coins, which were heavy and gray. He turned accusingly to the girl. "But why hastest thou turnething my coinery into yon worthless leadishness?" (Bogbrush forgot how to speak properly when he was more confused than usual.)

Laughing, Diphtheria snapped her fingers. A burst of red smoke appeared. Bogbrush jumped back again. "Look again!" she said. The barbarian looked. The bag was full of gold once more.

"But how?" he asked, his mouth hanging open in astonishment.

"The flash is iron pyrites and magnesium powder, plus a bit of something for color," answered

Diphtheria. "The rest of it's just a trick. I keep a bag of lead in one of my travel chests just to do that routine. People get distracted by the smoke and don't see me swap the two purses. Nobody notices if the purses aren't quite the same because they are looking for the gold!"

Sneaky grinned. "That's nothin' special. Why, I can turn anythin' I drink into pee!" Bogbrush would have asked questions about Sneaky's own trick, but suddenly there was a tremendous yell from nearby. A burly man with a red face shouted, "That's my cart! Stop him!" A huge crowd of men and boys, waving clubs and pitchforks came around a corner. A man in a blue helmet was blowing a whistle. They were coming for Bogbrush and his new friends.

"I shall hold back this mob of robbers!" cried Bogbrush as he pulled Headlopper from its scabbard. But Diphtheria grabbed him and hauled him backward by his hair.

"Ow! No fair!" shouted Bogbrush. I'd have said "squealed," but — as we know — barbarian heroes never squeal. He shouted in quite a high-pitched way, though.

A huge rock landed exactly on the spot where Bogbrush had been standing. A few smaller ones came hurtling through the air. One caught him on the forehead, and he fell back, dazed. "I am slain! I die bravely," he said woozily.

"No you don't," replied Diphtheria as she dragged the huge barbarian onto the "borrowed" cart.

Sneaky smacked the donkey forward. "Gotta avoid them mobs of robbers," he said. "Especially the ones wiv' the blue 'elmets. Right nasty, they can be."

The animal lumbered into a trot, and the robbers kept running, hurling rocks. Sneaky stayed low and urged the donkey onward. Nobby (who had been nosing through some interesting garbage in the ditch) looked around, shook his head in disgust and ambled after the cart.

"Wasn't that jolly!" said Diphtheria. "Every day is an adventure. Let's find another place to be."

Bogbrush nodded, still seeing stars. If this was how heroic quests began, he was ready.

CHAPTER 16

(I'm on to my last foot now.)

Sneaky said that you could find a merchant caravan along the Great South Road. They came along every half hour, as buses would if they'd been invented yet. He was right.

Bogbrush had never seen a caravan and thought it might be a giant monster with three heads that breathed fire. He was ready to slay it the moment it came into sight.

"Don't do that, Bogbrush," said Diphtheria. "It'll be messy, and then there will be all sorts of explaining to do."

The caravan was actually a long line of wagons, carts, donkeys, ponies and an animal Bogbrush had never seen before. It was like a big goat without horns, but it had a mountain growing out of its back. The beast had an unfriendly look to it, and seemed to be chewing something it didn't like the taste of.

"What is that creature?" asked Bogbrush. "It appeareth like a monster, yet it beareth bags." The creature was loaded down with leather sacks.

"That is a giant eastern hump-hamster," declared Sneaky. "Very dangerous!"

Diphtheria laughed, and smacked Sneaky across the shoulder. He almost fell out of the cart. But she didn't tell Bogbrush what the animal really was.

POP QUIZ! *What do you think the animal was?*

a) a giant eastern hump-hamster
b) a dromedary camel
c) a Bactrian camel
d) two men in a ridiculous costume
e) an elephant traveling in disguise

The caravan master wore a turban and a beard down to his enormous belly. He was happy to have another cart traveling with his party.

"I have need of a mighty thew'd guard, for our last one had a problem with arrows."

"What sorteth of problem?" asked Bogbrush.

"He had about ten of them sticking in him when I last saw him," replied the caravan master.

ONE WORD WITH TWO MEANINGS: That's party *as in "group of people," not* party *as in paper hats and being sick from too much cake.*

That didn't bother Bogbrush. He didn't have any arrows sticking in him, so that was all right.

The master went on. "And a thief! I shall make you chief of security. That means your job is to stop all the other thieves, since you know what they will be up to."

"What if I don't?" asked Sneaky.

"Then I'll get the guard to chop your head off!" declared the caravan master.

Bogbrush looked at his new friend as if he was measuring Sneaky's collar size. "Sorry, but I'd have to do it. It's all part of my job now," he said. The thief huffed a bit.

"And a female entertainer," continued the caravan master. "A lovely peach of the —"

"Don't even think about it!" snapped Diphtheria. "I am a respectable vocalist and actress, as well as a student of alchemy."

"Right," said the caravan master. "We travel to Scrofula, and the lands beyond."

"Scrofula will be fine," said Sneaky. "Just give me a moment to pee."

SCROFULA: *a great city, capital of Eczema, famous for its university, its temples, its palaces and its skin diseases. The sort of place you might go if you were seeking your fortune, or if angry people were after you.*

And so they went on, across deep rivers, vast mountain chains, treacherous swamps and dark, brooding forests. It was the sort of place where evil things could surprise an unwary traveler. As he scanned the landscape with his sharp eyes, Bogbrush thought about outlaws lurking behind trees, vicious wolves waiting to attack and all the things he liked about turnips.

CHAPTER 17
(This shoe is stuck.)

Bogbrush was cleaning Nosebiter as he rode along. He had decided that when he pulled the famous axe out of the stone, he'd still keep Nosebiter for everyday hacking and slaying. The other one would be for weekends and special occasions.

Nobby didn't like it when Bogbrush held a really big axe blade *quite* so close to his ears. He tried to walk carefully, without going over any bumps in the road.

Just then there was a scream, and a hail of arrows, stones, javelins and — surprisingly — rubber duckies came flying toward him.

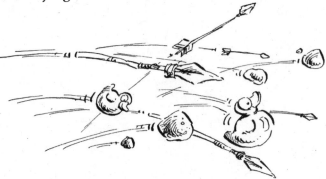

"Ayyyyeeee!" shouted a voice. *Thwack!* went an arrow into Bogbrush's turnip pouch. *Boing!* was the noise of a lump of granite hitting his helmet.

"Bandits!" shouted Sneaky. "Brigands!" said someone else. "Footpads!" called out a third, for the caravan had a dictionary open at the page marked *outlaws*.

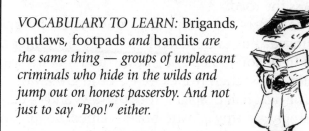

VOCABULARY TO LEARN: Brigands, outlaws, footpads *and* bandits *are the same thing — groups of unpleasant criminals who hide in the wilds and jump out on honest passersby. And not just to say "Boo!" either.*

Bogbrush thought about it for a moment and decided they might possibly be under attack.

Since he hadn't chopped anyone into dog meat for days and days, it would be a welcome change if a band of outlaws was to suddenly attack the caravan. The newcomers had been hiding among the rocks where the Great South Road went through a ravine. But Bogbrush

REMEMBER what a ravine is? Chapter three, or five. It's like a chasm, sort of. Anyway, the road went along the bottom of one. An ideal place for bandits. Or girl scouts selling cookies. Yum. Cookies …

wanted to be sure they weren't just — for instance — a troop of girl scouts waiting to sell delicious cookies to passersby.

Bogbrush was riding Nobby at the front of the caravan. He was the first to spot four trees lying across the road.

"Yon trees are sleeping in our path!" he announced. But even *he* realized, after a moment, that trees don't sleep lying down, and that the axe marks across their trunks were a dead giveaway.

The next hail of spears, rocks, arrows and — surprisingly — tiny plastic boats helped Bogbrush decide that something was definitely up. The screaming made it certain.

Plus the sudden appearance of dozens of ugly men in unattractive clothing, with poor dental care and curiously misspelled tattoos. They bore spears, knives, clubs and axes. One — for reasons of his own — carried a bundle of bathtub toys.

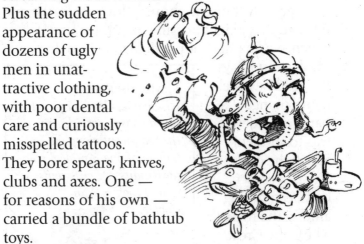

"Eeeeyaaagh!" screamed the bandits as they rushed out of the cover of boulders.

"Eeeeyaaagh!" screamed the caravan drivers, merchants, helpers, loaders and especially Sneaky.

Bogbrush didn't say "Eeeeyaaagh!"' at all but
flung Gutripper at the largest, ugliest, nastiest out-
law of them all. The giant spear lived up to its
name. The man flopped about, screaming something about "My guts, my guts!" After a while (to
everyone's relief) he ceased all the screaming and
the flopping. Bogbrush made a mental note to be
sure to collect Gutripper at the end of the day's fun.
He took Headlopper in one hand and Nosebiter in
the other.

All the outlaws tried the cunning trick of running around Bogbrush to find somebody else to
fight. But it didn't fool Bogbrush. Well, not for very
long.

The caravan master was trying to get the wagons
into a circle, the way they do in old western movies.
Since nobody had ever seen a western movie, the
drivers weren't doing very well. The camels refused
to have anything to do with the idea. An old lady
was standing on her cart, hitting outlaws with a
shovel. She seemed skillful at it, as if she'd done this
sort of thing before. A potter was using his fine

cooking pots as missiles. He had an excellent throwing arm. But most of the people weren't behaving like heroes; they seemed content with screeching and hiding and generally not being brave at all. The outlaws were winning.

Bogbrush wasn't putting up with that. He waded into the battle, slicing to his left and hacking to his right. Arms and legs went flying, men went slumping, blood went gushing. It was extremely messy, and *unsuitable for children under fourteen unless accompanied by an adult.*

Diphtheria was standing on top of the "borrowed" cart, hurling boxes at the attackers. She kept checking to see that they didn't contain anything breakable and scientific, which slowed things down quite a lot. But her aim was good, and she kicked anyone who got too close. After the first few fell down, clutching their noses and other vital organs, the outlaws left her alone. Sneaky was hiding under the cart.

Farther back in the caravan, someone was throwing lightning bolts at the brigands. Bogbrush didn't have time to watch — what with the hacking and slaying — but he knew what it meant. A magician! Or a really low black cloud! But probably a magician. A magician who didn't aim very well because, just as Bogbrush was happily slicing and dicing his way through a convenient bunch of bandits, a lightning bolt came straight toward him.

There was a sizzling noise and the whiff of roasting meat. Bogbrush thought it smelled delicious, just for a moment. Then he realized that the roasting meat was himself. Suddenly everything went black.

CHAPTER 18

(Now the left shoe is finally off.
What's that rattling around inside?)

Bogbrush dreamed he was in the hall of heroes. Dead heroes. His grandfather had told him that when barbarian warriors die, they go to a place where there is feasting all day, and fighting too, and much slaying.

"When it's time to feast some more, them as was slain in today's fighting put their heads back on, shovel their guts back inside and have a beer with them what killed 'em." That's how Bumrash had explained it. The place was called — what was it called? Hogwalla. Or Marshmalla? Bogbrush couldn't remember.

POP QUIZ: The Vikings had a name for the place where slain warriors went when they died. It was called

a) Hogwalla
b) Marshmalla
c) Valhalla
d) Walla Walla
e) Vanilla

In his dream, Bogbrush was fighting a huge, bearded warrior in golden armor. He swung Nosebiter and sliced off the fellow's leg. The warrior grinned, took his own axe and cleaved Bogbrush's left leg clean off into the distance. Bogbrush was surprised by this. It didn't seem to hurt, but standing up was difficult. He balanced on his right foot, swung Nosebiter again and smote the golden warrior's left arm into some nearby bushes. This didn't bother the man at all, for he thrust with his spear and stabbed it through the barbarian so that the point came out the other side.

Bogbrush didn't feel any pain from having a spear stuck right through him. It wasn't nearly as inconvenient as he might have expected. He swung Nosebiter again, and it bit the warrior's nose right off. In his other hand he held Headlopper, so he took the hint and lopped. The golden warrior's head bounced across the lawn.

"Good one, Bogbrush!" said the head. "Lovely swordplay. Time for more feasting?"

And with that, the remaining parts of his body picked up the missing arm and leg, clicked them both back into place and went over to collect the severed head and nose.

Bogbrush found that he could pull out the spear and fit his own leg back into place. It snapped back into position. There wasn't any blood messing up his chain mail, so he didn't have to wash before dinner. We all know that boys hate to wash their hands before dinner.

Bogbrush was enjoying Hogwalla. Or Vanilla. Whichever. There was plenty of ale, pork, beef, ale, goose, ale and all the turnips he could eat. That's a lot of turnips, I can tell you.

So Bogbrush wasn't very happy when a hand shook him by the shoulder, and a female voice said, "Are you awake, then?"

CHAPTER 19

(It's just a penny. I was hoping for a quarter.)

The woman's face was in shadow, but Bogbrush knew from her shawl and raven black hair that she had to be a witch. She held a bottle toward him.

EVERY DAY CAN BE HALLOWEEN!
We know that ravens are, in fact, black.
So are soot, ink, many shoes and my cat
Elmore. And yet, if I wrote that a witch's
hair was "shoe black," none of you would
think it was spooky at all.

"Witch!" yelled Bogbrush, dashing the bottle from her hand. "I shall not drink thy foul potion!"

"I didn't want you to drink it," said the woman. "I was going to rub it on those nasty burn marks on your arms. It's a lotion, not a potion."

THEY RHYME, BUT THEY'RE
DIFFERENT: Lotions you rub on,
potions you drink. Oceans you
swim in. The Locomotion was a
dance, popular in 1962.

"Who art thou, witch?" demanded Bogbrush. The witch laughed. Not cackled, like a proper witch, but laughed. Her voice was familiar.

"It's me, Bogbrush," said Diphtheria. "I've been looking after you for three days. Using all my alchemist's arts to cure you. That lightning bolt has muddled your brains."

"Thee looketh different," said Bogbrush. "Is it a spell?"

"No, it's a wig," Diphtheria said with a laugh. "I've got lots of them. This is my Easi-Care traveling wig, no curling needed." She pulled off the wig and threw it at Bogbrush. She had short dark hair underneath.

"Thy hair! It flies!" Bogbrush didn't understand the idea of a wig at all. Diphtheria reached into a box and pulled on the long blond wig she'd worn when she met him.

"Oh, there thou art!" he said. "There was magic afoot! Great sorcery!"

Diphtheria shook her head, smiling. "Just as long as you are feeling better. I was very worried. When Zeldar the Mage hurled his lightning bolt, he slew twelve outlaws. Fried them to a crisp. You were found at the bottom of a heap of frizzled bandits. That amulet must have saved your life. I thought you were dead."

"Not I!" declared Bogbrush. "I am a mighty hero!" He stood up. "I have a bone to pick with this Zeldar of whom thou speaketh."

But he picked no bones with Zeldar, because he fell over and began to snore again.

SAYING OF THE DAY: a bone to pick
— *this means to disagree with someone. I have no idea why people say this. It's not as though we're cavemen.*

CHAPTER 20

(That's all my fingers and toes counted.)

Zeldar was very sorry about the lightning bolt. Really.

"I'm very sorry about the lightning bolt, Bogbrush. I really am," he said. "I saw all those bandits in one clump of banditry, and what else could I do? I had no idea you were amongst them. None at all. Have a cigar!"

Zeldar had invented cigars. One day they might make him famous, if they caught on. Bogbrush ate the cigar in one mouthful. It was horrible. "Got any turnips?" he asked.

The sorcerer was a tall, thin man with a stoop; his face was old but his hair was glossy black. Another earwig? wondered Bogbrush. Will it fly?

WORD OF THE DAY: sorcerer — *a magician, wizard, mage, conjurer, illusionist or magic user. Someone who can pull a rabbit out of a hat without previously owning a rabbit — or possibly even a hat.*

They were seated around a campfire. The caravan had not been attacked by bandits that day. Or trolls, giants, dragons, or those animals that make a nasty smell when you startle them. Bogbrush didn't know what they were called.

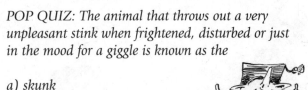

You could tell Bogbrush was feeling better because he was disappointed that there had been no fighting all day.

The caravan master had announced they were more than halfway to Scrofula, so they were celebrating with a feast. There was rich red wine, roasted meat and music. Diphtheria was dancing as she sang the always-popular "You May Be a Goblin but You're Mine." She wore her very best shiny silver dress and a bright red wig that flashed in the firelight. And about ten pounds (or 4.5 kilograms, metric readers) of cheap jewelry.

Zeldar the Mage was watching her with interest. With a lot of interest. After a while, he spoke. "Bogbrush, O mighty barbarian. This woman, this Diphtheria. She is yours, am I right?"

Bogbrush replied, "She is her own. We be just friends. She hath potioned and lotioned me back to health. She is an alchemist."

Zeldar snorted. "Alchemist, indeed! Why would a beautiful girl claim such absurd skills?" He leaned forward. "Bogbrush, I am a mighty sorcerer. I scorn this female alchemist of which you speak. And yet —"

His eyes flashed in a way that Bogbrush didn't like.

"I will have thou knowing that Diphtheria can indeed turn lead into gold, for I have seen it done, yea, with mine own eyes. And mine own gold!" declared the mighty barbarian. He had, too. Diphtheria had told him it was all a trick, but he couldn't see how. Anyway, he wanted to let this fellow know that Diphtheria was not to be insulted.

"Really? I would wish the alchemist girl for mine own belonging. What would you take for her?" demanded the sorcerer.

"Er, what?" said Bogbrush.

"Money! Power! Turnips! What would you want so that I can take the girl? I am a mighty worker of magic. I can give you all your heart desires!" replied Zeldar.

"But —" Bogbrush was speechless. This wicked man thought he could buy Diphtheria!

"All right, then, Bogbrush," said Zeldar the Mage. "I'll ask her myself."

The song ended and Zeldar walked over to speak with Diphtheria. They talked in low voices for a few moments. Then Bogbrush heard a loud smack, and Zeldar hit the floor with a crash.

CHAPTER 21
(Huh, I don't know what to do now ...)

"I can't believe that man," said Diphtheria as they resumed their journey the following day. "Cheeky devil wanted to buy me for my alchemistical abilities." Bogbrush didn't know what this meant.

"Turning lead into gold. That's what all these old men want," she fumed.

"He is a foul villain," agreed Bogbrush.

"He's a sly devil," said Sneaky. "You should watch your step, Dippy. I 'eard 'im going on about how 'the wench shall regret that slap,' after you stormed away."

"I'm not scared of him," snorted Diphtheria. "And don't call me Dippy, or I'll slap you as well."

"I'm just sayin'," replied the thief.

They traveled on, with Bogbrush explaining what he planned to do when he became the True King of Scrofula. Everyone would have their very own hamster (or camel), and turnips would always be half price. He would be beloved by all his adoring people, and there would be statues of King Bogbrush on every corner, made of ice cream.

Nobody wanted to point out the problems with statues made of ice cream. It would take too much explaining.

The caravan was now trundling through a range of great jagged mountains. Bogbrush rode at the front with Nobby wheezing along beneath him. He was looking out for bandits, trolls and dragons on the road ahead. They would have to deal with the mighty barbarian before they could reach the wagons!

So the ambushers tricked him, by waiting for him to *go past* before leaping down from the rocks beside the track. They hadn't been there when Bogbrush rode by. But now, he knew from the yelling, screaming and savage howling behind him — and that was just from Sneaky — that the wagons were being attacked. The mighty warrior turned around in his saddle (almost kicking Nobby in the head) and saw that these were not bandits, trolls, dragons or anything else on his list of "things that might attack you, so watch carefully!" but ape-men.

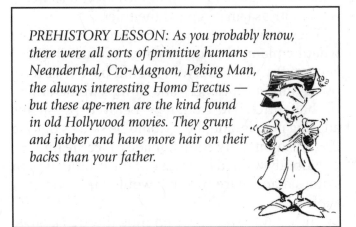

PREHISTORY LESSON: As you probably know, there were all sorts of primitive humans — Neanderthal, Cro-Magnon, Peking Man, the always interesting Homo Erectus — but these ape-men are the kind found in old Hollywood movies. They grunt and jabber and have more hair on their backs than your father.

"They are attackething the wagons," said Bogbrush to his horse. Nobby, being smarter than his owner, had already turned to gallop back. Er, waddle back.

But before the mighty barbarian hero could wade in with axe and sword, lopping and smiting and all that sort of thing, the attackers had gone. "Done a bunk," as his grandfather would have said.

PHRASE OF THE DAY: done a bunk — *this is not the same as* built a bunk. *The first implies leaving in a hurry with pursuers chasing. The other involves making a two-decker bed, which is very useful, etc., but will mean that even the slowest pursuer can catch up.*

There was not an ape-man to be seen anywhere.

"It was a hit-and-run job," said the caravan master. "They took my turban." He was bald underneath, his scalp a sickly white color compared with the tan of his face. "Good thing I've a spare."

"They took my best kitchen knives," said a woman who sold kitchenware.

"They stole my red cloak," complained a man who made wooden bowls.

"They took a very valuable book, *Illusions and Delusions*," said Zeldar the Mage. "And a wand of power. Three phials of magic powders. A scroll of spells. And a bedroom slipper."

Sneaky appeared from under a pile of sacks, where he'd been hiding. His expression was very sour.

"I 'ate to say this, Bogbrush. They've took Diphtheria."

CHAPTER 21 AGAIN

(I am stuck now, as I have no more feet.)

The ape-men had been gone for just a few minutes. "We must rescue Diphtheria!" said Bogbrush. "Who wilt come with me?"

There was muttering and a lot of excuses. "Got to get the caravan moving again," said the caravan master. "All my stuff got messed up," said a merchant. "The dog ate my homework," said another.

Bogbrush looked at Sneaky. Sneaky sighed. "All right, all right. I'll come along. I'm good at following trails. Looking for broken twigs and footprints in mud, that sort of thing. They teach all that at thievin' school. But you do know I'm a complete coward, don't you?"

"Yes," said Bogbrush. "Thou art yellow throughout."

"Just as long as you know," said Sneaky.

"We'll go on foot," said Bogbrush as he handed Nobby's reins to a small girl (who said "Coo! It's Cuddles!" and jumped on the pony's back). "For ape-men travel over country too rough for a steed."

"Plus I ain't got no steed anyway, and I ain't runnin' to keep up," sniffed Sneaky. "Besides, we needs to be cunning, and 'orses make a lot of noise."

Bogbrush thought they should travel light. He put a few turnip sandwiches and a leather bottle of only slightly dirty water in his pouch. The potter's wife gave him a chewy meat stick she called "spamican."

WORD OF THE DAY: The native peoples of North America ate something called pemmican made from dried deer, moose or buffalo meat pounded together with fat and berries. It was popular as traveler's food. The potter's wife, being short on deer, moose or buffalo meat, used a canned product called SPAM®. Your grocery store will stock it. Try it! (This message brought to you by SPAM® Lovers of the World.)

"It's good for journeys in the wilds because it lasts a long time," she said.

"Thou meanest it does not spoil in the heat?" asked Bogbrush.

"No, I mean it's so tough you can't swallow it," replied the potter's wife.

The mighty barbarian decided to leave his horned helmet, his axe and his spear in the cart. "Don't touch my stuff!" he told everyone. "I'll be back." He pointed to a boy with freckles. "Thou art in charge."

Nobody was about to touch Bogbrush's stuff, except Sneaky, and Sneaky was going along for the trip.

"The primitive savages went that way," announced Zeldar. "I saw them go." He pointed dramatically toward a mountain in the distance.

"And don't be all day," said the caravan master. "I don't pay you to be wasting time rescuing damsons who have been foolish enough to get kidnapped by ape-men."

DAMSONS are a kind of soft fruit, like plums. Nobody wastes valuable time rescuing endangered fruit. The caravan master means damsels, young women who spend a lot of time "in distress" (or dat dress).

Bogbrush gave him a dirty look. The caravan master didn't seem to notice. So Bogbrush smacked him on the head with the flat side of his sword. The caravan master definitely noticed that.

"You're fired!" he whimpered when he woke up. But Bogbrush and Sneaky had already gone.

CHAPTER 23

(Did I miss one? A chapter, not a foot.)

The country was rough and tangly with big rocks and gnarled old trees that brushed the ground.

WORD OF THE DAY: gnarled — pronounced "narld." Sort of twisty, in an elderly way. Use it today, as in "You are looking pretty gnarled, Mrs. Smith. Is there a test in class this morning?"

Bogbrush and Sneaky climbed over rocks and under trees for hours.

"No footprints," said Sneaky. "I wish we had a dog."

"I like dogs," replied Bogbrush. "I like cats, too, but what I really want is some guinea pigs. Guinea pigs are cuddly."

This surprised Sneaky. He'd have expected that Bogbrush's idea of a good pet would be something large and man-eating.

"I'm not talking about pets, you idio — barbarian warror!" snapped Sneaky. "A dog to sniff the scent for us. Follow the trail. Maybe do a bit of biting as well."

Bogbrush thought about that as they wandered around the tangly parts some more.

> PET-OWNER'S ADVICE: Guinea pigs are small rodents, suitable animals for children to keep. They are completely unskilled at tracking, detecting scents and attacking enemies. But they are cuddly. (A very large picture of a guinea pig must be inserted here —I insist.)
>
>

"It's no use," said Sneaky. "We've passed that old tree three times now. Going around in circles. Let's go back to the caravan and start again."

Which was a good idea, except that they couldn't find the caravan. What they did find was a silver bracelet with emeralds on it. Fake silver. Emeralds made of paste.

> IMITATION JEWELS are made of some sort of paste. Not the sort you use in craft projects or the stuff your little brother likes to eat. Some other kind.

"Forsooth!" said Bogbrush. "Someone has lost a bangle!"

"Nobody 'as *lost* a bangle," replied Sneaky. "Diphtheria 'as deliberately *dropped* a bangle. Let's see if she's left any more for us to follow."

The trail was very easy to track. It wasn't that the ape-men left a lot of banana skins or broken branches. They hadn't. But Diphtheria had dug her heels into the dirt whenever she could, leaving deep gouges in the path. Every so often there was a piece of cheap jewelry on a rock or hanging from a tree.

"'Tis easy!" said Bogbrush. "We just started off in the wrong direction."

"Yes we did, didn't we?" said Sneaky, and added sarcastically, "I wonder who pointed out which way we should go?"

Bogbrush pondered this. Had Sneaky lost his memory? And — now that the mighty thew'd warrior thought about it — who *had* told them which way to go?

CHAPTER 25

(Or 24, maybe. I am confused.)

The primitive savages stopped at a clearing in the woods to make camp for the night. They began making a fire by rubbing sticks together, the way boy scouts are supposed to do. If there had been any boy scouts around, the ape-men might have rubbed *them* together to start the fire instead.

They also tied Diphtheria — now very short of bangles and bracelets — to a tree.

"Watch where you are putting your hairy hands!" said Diphtheria crossly.

"Ook! Eek!" replied the ape-man with the hairy hands.

Actually, they all had hairy hands. Diphtheria was just singling out the one nearest her. He was larger than the others and had feathers stuck on his head with gum. It was an elegant look. Anyone could tell he was the chief.

Out among the trees, Sneaky pulled Bogbrush into the cover of a boulder. "Shh!" he whispered. "Let's listen first, and make a plan to rescue Dippy."

"I have a plan," said Bogbrush. "I slay these man-beasts with mighty blows from Headlopper. You free Diphtheria. Then we leave."

"Well, yeah, it's a good plan," admitted Sneaky. "But let's count the ape-men. Just to see 'ow many you've got to slay while I'm doing the untying."

This was a cunning scheme, indeed, thought the barbarian. Count them first. Bogbrush held up both hands to see if he could do this. He couldn't. There were more ape-men than fingers to count them on.

Sneaky watched the campsite carefully. He saw something moving in the forest. "Psst, Bogbrush!" whispered the thief. A man emerged from the forest and advanced into the clearing. He was tall but stooping and wore a wizard's robe. It was Zeldar the Mage.

"I had not expected that!" said Bogbrush.

"I 'ad," replied Sneaky.

A second figure approached from another direction. He greeted Zeldar with a wave and a shout. "Hail, brother!" Bogbrush couldn't identify the new arrival. Sneaky recognized him, though. He shook his head in amazement.

"I 'adn't expected *that*," muttered Sneaky.

Bogbrush peered at the two men who were shaking hands by the light of the campfire. "Why hast Zeldar appearethed here? And who is yon other fellow?" he asked, full of questions. "Why cometh they to this place?"

Sneaky reached into his pouch and pulled out a sling. "Let's find out."

WEAPON OF THE WEEK: The sling is a leather strap that shoots a pebble or a metal ball when you spin it over-arm and release the missile. It can shoot as far as a bow and put your eye out. Or worse. This is not a toy! Don't try this at home!

Bogbrush expected Sneaky to hurl a shot at one of the men. Instead, he slung a pebble, not hard, at one of the ape-men bringing more wood for the fire.

"Ook! Eek!" cried the ape-man, rubbing his head. All his friends ran over, eeking and ooking to see what had happened.

Meanwhile — and this actually was cunning — Sneaky led Bogbrush around the edge of the clearing. The mighty warrior was amazed at how fast and light the little thief could be. It was almost as if he was invisible as he flitted from tree to rock to bush. His gray clothes concealed him completely. Bogbrush tried hard to follow. A branch cracked under his size 17 $^1/_2$ foot.

"Shh! You big oaf — er, hero!" whispered Sneaky.

They slid forward into the cover of a large oak tree. The campfire was now just a few paces away. Diphtheria was tied up to another oak tree in the center of the clearing. She had a lot to say, but none of it is suitable for young readers.

While the ape-men rushed to see what had happened to their comrade, Zeldar the Mage spoke with the newcomer. Bogbrush suddenly realized who the other man was — Lucidar, the cardsharp! He and Zeldar were indeed brothers.

"They are brothers!" announced Bogbrush in astonishment. "I have brothers! Although mine are yokels and much tinier than myself!"

Sneaky winced at the barbarian's booming voice and idiotic comments. "I wonder what they are up to?" he whispered.

"I could go and ask them!" replied Bogbrush far too loudly.

"Shh! No, let's just listen a few moments," said the thief. "And please, please, try to make less noise than an angry elephant on a bad day."

So Sneaky listened as Zeldar and Lucidar talked, and Bogbrush was careful not to break anything, or yell, or do any of the many things he so often did that made more noise than an angry elephant on a bad day.

Suddenly he felt a hand tap him on the back —

WORD OF THE DAY: cliffhanger —
a chapter or an episode that ends with
a dramatic moment designed to make
the reader want to find out what happens
next! Even if what comes next is a
complete letdown —

CHAPTER 20-LOTS

(That's about it, right?)

"It's just me, Bogbrush," whispered Sneaky. "I 'ad to find a tree to pee behind."

(See — that was a really crummy cliffhanger! Didn't I warn you?)

They listened to the evil sorcerer talking evilly to his equally evil brother as they hatched their evil schemes in an evil way.

"This is a fine plan," said Lucidar. "How much are you paying those beast-men?"

"I promised their chief as much fire powder as he wants," replied Zeldar. "And a few worthless trinkets. In return, we get the beautiful Diphtheria. The barbarian tells me she is an alchemist who can turn base metals into gold. We will travel to distant Tzing or legendary Kalash, where nobody knows us for the notorious villains we are" — insert evil chuckling here — "and we will force her to make us rich with newly made gold. She'll never escape from us there!"

Bogbrush whispered to Sneaky. "Where be those places?"

"Shh!" replied the thief. "Foreign, faraway places I've only 'eard of."

It was probably a good thing that Bogbrush did not make the connection between Zeldar's description of "the beautiful Diphtheria" who would make them rich in "distant Tzing or legendary Kalash" and any actual plan to abduct her to some far-off place and force her to make gold for them. That would have upset him a lot, and he would have been unable to resist his natural urge to scream a stirring battle cry, pull out his sword and rush forward against Zeldar, Lucidar and an as-yet-uncounted number of hairy ape-men.

Well, wouldn't we all? I know I would. But it was not yet time for slicing off ears, hacking off limbs and blood-drenched butchery in general (not that I am good at that sort of thing myself).

The two evil men continued their conversation. "Aye!" said Lucidar. "A fortune for ourselves, and rich revenge on Diphtheria! The girl ruined my brilliant scheme with the cards and dice!"

"Brother Lucidar," said Zeldar. "If thou hadst studied in school, as I did, thou couldst be a great sorcerer today. Yet, thou didst goof off and get D minuses, and thou knowest only enough spells to cheat at games. Even then, thou needest marked cards and loaded dice to make thy living."

EDUCATION MATTERS! Don't be like Lucidar and waste your learning years! Study hard and become an evil sorcerer like Zeldar!

Lucidar snorted but hung his head a little.

"Yet, brother," said Zeldar, "thou chose our victim well, and the fortune we get from her wilt make us rich!"

Diphtheria could hear everything they were saying. "BLEEP your DELETED and CENSORED lightning bolt up your BLEEP BLEEP!" she said.

"Cut out her tongue before we take her?" said Lucidar.

"I think so," replied Zeldar.

That was too much for Bogbrush. Diphtheria needed her tongue. How else would she eat ice cream? And what if she wanted to pull funny faces? He snorted in disgust and began to draw Headlopper from its scabbard, but Sneaky stopped him. "Not yet," he whispered. "They've got to get Dippy away from 'ere, and then we can make our move. When there's not forty-three ape-men waiting to do us in."

"Do us in?" said Bogbrush.

Sneaky made the international sign for a cut throat. "Oh," replied Bogbrush. Forty-three was far more than he could fight at once. Or count, even. Especially since he had boots on and couldn't count his toes as well as his fingers.

"How do we get the girl away with us?" asked Lucidar. "She won't cooperate, and we can't put her in a bag."

"We can, brother. I have a shrinking spell that will reduce her to the size of a sparrow, and a cage to carry her," replied Zeldar.

That, too, was evil, thought Bogbrush. He did not think Diphtheria would enjoy sitting on a perch or eating seeds out of a little plastic cup.

While the barbarian brooded over the details of birdcage amenities, his companion was still planning the rescue of Diphtheria.

A NOTE FROM THE AUTHOR: As the writer of this fine book, I feel I should point out to budding authors that for every big, stupid muscle-head in your story, you need someone with actual smarts to figure things out. Otherwise it's just blood and gore and severed body parts, page after page. Well, yes, I like that, too, but your publisher will fuss about it.

Sneaky looked carefully at Zeldar. The evil magician was carrying a bag. "I bet ee's got that fire powder in 'is sack," whispered the thief to Bogbrush. "And the other stuff to pay the ape-men. Let's see what we can do with that."

CHAPTER 9

(I liked Chapter 9,
so I am using it again.)

The ape-men had decided that the one who had
been hit by the pebble was not going to die, and
that he'd simply been stung by a wasp. Or something like that. Who understands what ape-men
are saying? They all came back to the campfire,
anyway.

The chief — the big one with the feathers in his
fur — approached Zeldar and his brother. Zeldar
stepped forward to greet him. His bag did not.
Sneaky had slipped ahead, cut the strap with a
stroke of a tiny blade, and was back behind the tree
in a flash. Bogbrush was impressed. Sneaky was
small, skinny, completely cowardly and totally
dishonest. But he was really good at stealing things.

*PARENTAL ALERT: Spend several long and
boring hours explaining to your children
that stealing is wrong! Just because
Sneaky is trying to save Diphtheria
from being kidnapped is no reason for
him to resort to stealing. Wrong! Wrong!
Wrong!*

"Greetings, O great chief," said Zeldar the Mage.

"Eeeky Ook!" said the ape-man chief. "Is catch female! Good! Swap for fire! Eek!"

Bogbrush was impressed that the chief spoke English. Sort of.

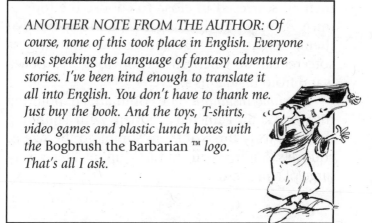

ANOTHER NOTE FROM THE AUTHOR: Of course, none of this took place in English. Everyone was speaking the language of fantasy adventure stories. I've been kind enough to translate it all into English. You don't have to thank me. Just buy the book. And the toys, T-shirts, video games and plastic lunch boxes with the Bogbrush the Barbarian ™ *logo. That's all I ask.*

"Yes, fire," said Zeldar. "The amazing secret of fire. Aren't you tired of making fire the old-fashioned way? With just a pinch of new *Magic Fire-Starting Powder* it's easy to light a candle, a bonfire — or set your enemy's barn alight! Accept no substitute! But wait, there's more! I have powder for many —"

He reached toward the strap of his bag. Actually it was just a strap. It held absolutely nothing on the other end.

"— er, many fires. My brother will show you an

amazing magical trick — er, spell — while I bring forth the wonderful gifts I have brought for you." Zeldar was patting all his pockets and looking at the ground behind him. He'd had the bag a moment ago.

"Pick a card, any card!" said Lucidar. The ape-men all squeezed in close to choose the four of mice. As they bunched together, all forty-three of them, Zeldar the Mage showed what a ruthless sorcerer can do when things go wrong. He drew a wand from inside his sleeve.

"*Diminuo Instantish!*" he commanded, pointing the wand at the gathered ape-men. With a blinding flash, all forty-three of them shrank to the size of squirrels. Squirrels all standing up, picking a very large playing card.

MAGICAL TERMINOLOGY *is always in a sort of fake Latin. We know this from popular children's books. It sounds more impressive than "Get Small Quick!" Find the biggest, most brutish kid in your class and command him to shrink, both in English and fake Latin. See which one works best!*

Behind the tree, Bogbrush and Sneaky looked on with amazement. Bogbrush thought that if he was shrunk so small, he'd *hardly* be able to do any barbarian heroics *at all.* He'd have to sharpen the edge of a teaspoon for a weapon, and get an egg cup for a helmet.

"Nice to see how far you can be trusted," said Diphtheria, narrowing her eyes at the sorcerer. "You'd sell your own grandmother if it suited you!"

"I did that already, when I was twelve," replied Zeldar. "Got four copper coins and a pork pie for her." He cackled in an evil way, as you'd expect him to do. "Lucidar, untie the girl."

Lucidar looked at his brother. "Aren't you going to make her tiny as well? She's a biter."

Zeldar rolled his eyes. "I have only the one spell at a time, fool! We'll just change the plan a little. Untie her before I lose patience with you!"

Diphtheria was a clever one, of course. Lucidar approached the oak carefully. First he stepped behind the tree and freed the cords around the singer's feet and waist. Then he came around the front, where her hands were tied. "Promise you won't bite?" he said.

"I promise I won't bite," said Diphtheria. "Look, no crossed fingers."

Then she kicked him hard under the old oak tree, and Lucidar fell to the ground whimpering. Like a little child, the spoiled kind who throw tantrums.

Zeldar laughed. Diphtheria realized he had other magic aside from the shrinking spell. She might be the person who could make him rich by alchemy, but Zeldar was in a very bad mood. You could tell that from his laugh. Sorcerers in bad moods are tricky to deal with. He might turn her into a toad or a pound of chopped liver, at least until he arrived in Kalash or Tzing or Winnipeg, wherever they might be. Diphtheria did not want to be turned into chopped liver.

CHAPTER 28
(That might actually be correct.
Who can say?)

Bogbrush stepped out from behind his tree. "I am Bogbrush, mighty barbarian warrior. Prepare to meet thy doom!" He had Headlopper in hand, his mighty thews glistened and he looked happy. This was exactly the sort of thing he'd been training for all his life. All that practicing on the turnips.

Zeldar the Mage laughed at him. The sorcerer pulled himself up to his full height. He was even taller than Bogbrush. He spread his arms out wide in a sweeping gesture of magic and laughed again.

"Bwa ha ha ha ha!"

This was how evil magicians laughed. How *many* evil magicians laughed. Because suddenly there were many, many Zeldars, all whirling around Bogbrush in a jabbering of Bwa-ha-ha-ing.

HOMEWORK: Go around the house yelling "Bwa ha ha ha ha!" until a member of your family stops you. Get five points for "Shut up, you annoying little monster!" Ten points if someone actually attempts to stuff something down your throat to keep you quiet.

The barbarian slashed at the Zeldar in front of him. There was a burst of light that almost blinded Bogbrush, and more laughter. It was becoming louder and more insane, stabbing his eardrums and screaming into his brain. There were Zeldars all around him, and, as Bogbrush swung his sword, each one exploded into flashes of light. And then there were even more, and the laughter grew even louder.

"BU-WAH HA HA HA HA!!"

Diphtheria kicked one of the Zeldars that came close to the tree, where she was still tied up. It was a good kick and produced another explosion. The insane chuckling went on and on, each *ha-ha* echoing against all the other *ha-ha-has*. Bogbrush was going mad. He put all his mighty strength into wild swings of the sword, enough to slice bison in half, if there were any. He stabbed deep enough to smash through fortress doors. He struck with the speed of a fat troll reaching for the last cupcake. It was no use. Each blow created more Zeldars, all laughing and spinning and — this was the worst part — sticking waggling fingers in their ears. They were teasing Bogbrush into insanity.

And then, one of the Zeldars stopped laughing, and said, "Ooff!" His hands reached back behind his head, his eyes crossed and he pitched forward onto his face. The other Zeldars stopped instantly, frozen with fingers in ears.

Sneaky stepped out from behind the tree, the sling in his hand. "Got 'im!" he said. "Pebble behind the left ear. Out like a light."

The other Zeldars flickered and faded into nothing.

"How did you know which one to shoot?" asked Diphtheria. She sounded impressed with Sneaky, which was something new.

"Pick a card, any card," said Sneaky. "'Ee was the only one who left any footprints as 'ee jumped up and down."

"Pick a card!" murmured Lucidar, still lying groggy on the ground.

Diphtheria stepped on his face. "Oh, sorry. That might hurt!" She looked at Bogbrush. "Are you going to chop off Zeldar's head, then?"

"Nay," replied Bogbrush. "It is not right to slay a man when he is down."

"Prop 'im up, then," said Sneaky. "Lean him against a tree stump."

Bogbrush shook his head. "The code of the Great Belch forbids it. 'Twould be wrong to slay him."

Diphtheria shook her head because her code said that a man who thinks he can kidnap you to make him rich may think the same thing another day.

FUN WITH ETHICS: When is it all right to chop off somebody's head?

a) When it's a fair fight with big swords. Or possibly axes.

b) When you are really, really annoyed with them, and your mother's not looking.

c) When you've got a new sword and want to try it out right now.

d) It's never right to decapitate anyone. Get the dictionary if you need to look up decapitate. *I try hard to educate today's young people. I believe children are our future.*

Diphtheria was almost certainly right about Zeldar, but she really didn't want to chop off his head herself. Nice girls don't do that sort of thing. Sneaky had another solution. "I think them ape-men may want to sort out the matter in their own way!"

The tiny ape-men rushed forward to where Zeldar lay. One of them picked up a rock with both hands. It was about the size of a walnut. He used it to smack Zeldar on the nose. Another was trying to sharpen a twig into a spear. The others were jumping on the sorcerer, shouting "Eek! Ook!" in high voices. "Make big again or we pull out all teeth! Ook!" shouted the chief. Really, he spoke well for an ape-man.

"Cut me loose, you idiots," said Diphtheria. "Let's go back to the caravan. And give Zeldar's bag of fire powder to the ape-men. I'm sure they can think of all sorts of interesting ways to use it."

CHAPTER 27

(Is there a rule that says
I can't go backward?)

Bogbrush had made many threats as to what would happen if anyone touched his belongings, so, of course, all the children of the caravan were wearing his armor, clambering on Nobby and threatening one another's vital parts with his weapons. Luckily, none of them was strong enough to swing Nosebiter or throw Gutripper. That could have been "very nasty," as Sneaky said. The boy that Bogbrush had asked to look after Nobby swore that it was nothing to do with him.

"I tol' 'em to leave it alone. I said you'd be mad at 'em!" he declared. Since he was wearing Bogbrush's helmet (which came down to his chin), it was hard to believe he was telling the truth.

"Good lad!" said Bogbrush with a smile,

slapping the boy on the back so that he flew five paces into a patch of mud. The other children decided that they didn't want Bogbrush to like them *too* much from now on.

The caravan master had "forgotten" that he'd fired Bogbrush. It seemed like the best thing to do when a huge barbarian returns with a rescued damson — er, damsel — and a big sword. And he didn't complain when Bogbrush decided that Zeldar's wagon now belonged to him and his friends.

"Someone must look after the 'orse," explained Sneaky. "Zeldar told us — mentioned in passing, as it were — that 'ee'd not be accompanying us on our journey."

The caravan master didn't argue.

Bogbrush was happy because he had freed his friend Diphtheria and vanquished an evil sorcerer. Diphtheria had taken charge of all the magic powders and sorcering gear from Zeldar's wagon for her alchemy research, so she was happy as well. They were in the cart, loaded high, with Diphtheria driving. Nobby was in the cart as well; he needed a rest after the children had spent all afternoon riding on his back.

Sneaky had immediately sold Zeldar's wagon and horse to the first merchant who showed an interest in them. He should have been happy, too, but he'd been disappointed by the lack of gold and jewels in the wagon. "They'd be mine, see, as is only right. Only 'ee ain't got 'ardly any."

"Do not grumble, dishonest friend," said Bogbrush. "For we are on a great adventure. Where is this caravan going to, again? I hast forgotten, in all the excitement!"

"Scrofula," said Diphtheria. "You are on a quest, remember? The legend of the True King? The Axe in the Stone?"

Bogbrush nodded. He *did* remember that part.

Diphtheria went on talking. "For myself, I intend to make them take me into the university. Or else."

"Or else you'll kick 'em where they don't like it," said Sneaky. "I intend to steal from rich Scrofulans who've never met a master thief like me before. Only they won't meet me, 'cos I'll 'ave cleared off with all their belongings!"

> SCROFULA: A great city, capital of Eczema, famous for its university, its temples, its palaces and its skin diseases. Mentioned in Chapter sixteen. Fourteen? Nine? Ages ago, really.

"They'll like that. A big city like Scrofula probably needeth more thieves," said Bogbrush. "And I shall pull the axe from the big rock, and be proclaimed True King of Scrofula!" He was so excited at these thoughts that he almost fell off the cart.

Diphtheria snorted. "You'll need someone to look after you. You're a danger to yourself, you are."

"A danger to everyone," said Bogbrush contentedly.

"This Axe in the Stone thing," said Sneaky. "You're sure you want to try it? The regent won't want you to succeed, you know."

"I am sure he'll be happy to find the True King," replied Bogbrush. "He can take some time off, go forth unto the beach, or pursue other hobbies for which he hath had little time."

"Yeah," said Sneaky, "only I think that actually ruling Scrofula with an iron hand is what 'ee does as a hobby."

"An iron hand? That I wouldst like to see!" answered the barbarian.

"You might get the chance," said Diphtheria darkly.

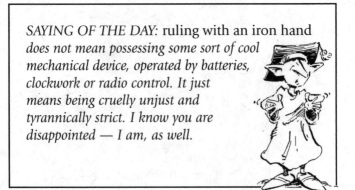

SAYING OF THE DAY: ruling with an iron hand *does not mean possessing some sort of cool mechanical device, operated by batteries, clockwork or radio control. It just means being cruelly unjust and tyrannically strict. I know you are disappointed — I am, as well.*

CHAPTER 20-10
(What?)

For days the caravan advanced along the road toward the south. Dust from the wagons in front of them covered the cart and everything inside it. Diphtheria handled the reins while Sneaky dozed between taking pee breaks. Bogbrush and Nobby ambled along behind the cart. Sometimes the barbarian rode the tiny pony, sometimes he carried him over his brawny shoulder. Sometimes both of them rode in the cart. It seemed only fair.

They had given up scouting ahead for trouble because trouble seemed to have no difficulty finding them up till now. Trouble did finally seem to be taking its coffee break for a while, at least until the gleaming towers of Scrofula came into sight.

Scrofula was the biggest city Bogbrush had ever seen. If there had been only a sandcastle model of Scrofula, it would have *still* been the biggest city that Bogbrush had ever seen. It would have taken him the whole day to kick over all the sandcastles.

The city was surrounded by a great wall. The only entrance was through a gatehouse guarded by soldiers — rough, rude men in bronze helmets and chain mail. They weren't paid very much, but they were allowed to be as rude as they liked. They liked to be very rude, indeed.

The caravan master had led the column of wagons, one behind the other, toward a massive gateway, where a sign said CUSTOMS in several languages — Tzinchi, Vulgarese, Inkomprehensive and French. The caravan master had to explain what he was bringing into the city, and pay tolls, tariffs and taxes.

TOLLS, TARIFFS AND TAXES: You'll find out about these when you get older. Basically, whatever you have, the government wants as much of it as they can get. Ask your dad about them if you want to hear him curse out loud!

Diphtheria had kept their cart well back in the procession of wagons, hoping to avoid any argument with the soldiers. She was wrapped in a blanket and wearing the ugliest wig she could find. The singer was trying to look as unattractive as she could. It wasn't really working. Sneaky told Bogbrush to stay quiet, sit still and look as stupid as he could.

"What meanest thou?" demanded the barbarian.

Sneaky rolled his eyes. "Just act normal. Only quiet normal, not slicing-people-into-bits normal."

A guard approached the cart. "Wotcha got there, darlin'?" he asked.

"Potions, young man," she answered in the voice of an old woman. "Ointments for rashes, medicines for upset stomachs, creams to rub on your pimples."

"Got any love charms?" asked the guard, "'Cos I'd put one on you."

"Give over," said Sneaky. "Leave 'er alone." He said this because he knew that Diphtheria would have a lot more to say, and it wouldn't be polite. She might kick him or punch him to let him know how she felt.

"Oh, yeah," replied the guard. "And 'oo would you be? Her *boyfriend*?" He said "boyfriend" in that way you've heard at school. You know, the way that says there's something wrong with you, or her, or both of you. Bullies practice saying things like that.

"We are Just Good Friends," announced Bogbrush. "There are no boyfriends here."

The guard was one of those annoying characters who thinks he's funny when he isn't. "So, are you saying you *aren't really a boy* then, youngster?"

Bogbrush's face turned red because he knew he was being insulted. He just wasn't sure exactly how. "I am a barbarian warrior. With a certificate and a magic amulet and everything."

The soldier laughed at him.

I'll bet you know what happened next —

CHAPTER 20-11

(I am getting the hang of this now.)

Well, you'd be wrong. Bogbrush did not pull out either Nosebiter or Gutripper and hack the rude (and, I think it's fair to say, stupid) guard into a dozen steaks, chops and the makings of sausages. He might have done that, but Sneaky laid a hand on him and whispered, "Easy, lad."

That, and Diphtheria smashed a massive vase over the soldier's head. He went down in a heap like a ton of wet fish.

You could tell that Diphtheria had done this sort of thing before, because she hopped down and — showing quite amazing strength — hoisted the unconscious guard into the back of the wagon in front of them. Sneaky pulled a sheet over him in a flash and kicked his helmet off into the gutter. The wagon was owned by two old women who spoke only in twitters and had a cargo of dried mammoth manure. The other guards weren't likely to look too carefully at their cart.

Diphtheria drove slowly through the gate while Sneaky whistled a favorite tune known as "My Love Smells like an Open Drain," which is no longer popular. Bogbrush stayed quiet, trying to think of a snappy comeback to the rude soldier. He would come up with something before breakfast tomorrow.

And then, they were inside the fabled city of Scrofula.

WORD OF THE DAY: fabled *means something, somewhere or someone mentioned in legend, myth or, er, fable. Atlantis, Xanadu and El Dorado are fabled cities. You can use it about your own hometown, if you like. I come from the Fabled City of Birmingham, for instance, as do the fabled heroes of legend, Duran Duran.*

"Forsooth, that building is many huts on top of one another!" marveled Bogbrush. He was impressed, although he wondered if they had been built that way by mistake. He made mistakes all the time, but he had never accidentally placed all the huts in his village on top of one another. His mom would yell if he did.

Diphtheria laughed. "It is five stories tall. There are bigger ones near the regent's palace," she said.

She knew right away that this was the wrong thing to say.

"Let us go there forthwith and right now," said Bogbrush. "And I shall get this Being the True King business sorted out."

"Are you sure you really want to?" asked Diphtheria doubtfully, although she knew the answer already. A smart person might have asked her what she was concerned about.

Bogbrush was not that person. "Aye!" he replied with hearty enthusiasm.

Diphtheria rolled her eyes in frustration.

"Well, can we stop for a pee break first?" asked Sneaky. "I'm dyin' to go."

Well, he was. Caravans don't have potties.

Ten minutes later they were parked outside a building that had *palace* written all over it. Not literally, of course, because palaces are classy joints and don't need to advertise. If it had a sign that said PALACE, it would have probably been a casino.

Sneaky was refused entry when he asked to "visit the gents' room." That's another thing about palaces. They won't let just anyone use the toilets.

"You can't park that ruddy great cart 'ere, darlin'," announced the soldier who had turned Sneaky away. Diphtheria glowered at him. She'd had enough of Scrofula's city guards. The man stepped back in fear. Diphtheria had a really terrifying glare when she wanted to. "It's the regent," he explained apologetically. "If it was up to me, you could leave it anywhere you liked. I'd hold the donkey for you. I'd give it an apple. I'd *buy* the apple."

The guard still didn't let Sneaky into the palace, though. The thief disappeared behind a marble column. He really needed to go right away.

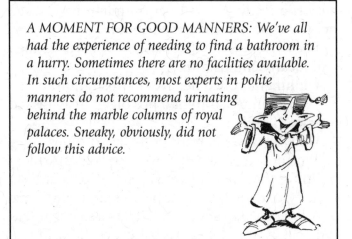

A MOMENT FOR GOOD MANNERS: We've all had the experience of needing to find a bathroom in a hurry. Sometimes there are no facilities available. In such circumstances, most experts in polite manners do not recommend urinating behind the marble columns of royal palaces. Sneaky, obviously, did not follow this advice.

With a fanfare of trumpets, the palace doors opened and a procession came out. A squad of marching soldiers emerged first, followed by a collection of people dressed in silks and furs, all chatting to one another in a way that said, "*We're* important and *you're* not." In the middle of the throng was a fancy sedan chair, held aloft by four massive, muscle-bound bearers. They wore yellow turbans, baggy pajama trousers of pink silk, and little striped vests over bare chests.

"Those be silly costumes," announced Bogbrush very loudly.

"Shh!" whispered Sneaky, who had returned from watering the column. "I think they already know that. I wouldn't go sayin' it too loud."

A man in purple robes and a big gold hat — almost a crown, but not quite — sat in the sedan chair. He was thin, with a long neck, and pimply. A midget perched behind him, peeling grapes and feeding them to him.

"More wed ones," he told the tiny grape peeler.

The bossy man smacked the little servant aside. "That was a gween gwape, you widiculous wascal!" The midget fell off the sedan chair and scurried away between the feet of the huge bearers. "Bwing another gwape peeler!"

"Nice man," said Diphtheria. She was being sarcastic.

CHAPTER 20-12

(Hey, this counting thing is easy!)

The procession processed out into the square, with burly soldiers pushing aside the crowd.

(This part is not completely true. When the soldiers came to Bogbrush and his friends, they looked up at him and decided to go and bully someone smaller and without quite so many weapons.)

Most of the people simply got knocked into the gutter as the regent yelled, "Move the wiffwaff out of my path!"

"Where goeth that skinny fellow in the high chair?" asked Bogbrush.

"That's the weegent," replied Sneaky. "Dunno where 'ee's off to, though. Let's follow 'im." He made a clicking noise that the donkey recognized as "Break is over, start pulling the $#%^&* cart again!"

WORD OF THE DAY: weegent — Sneaky is, of course, making fun of the regent's speech impediment, where he pronounces the letter r *as a* w. *This is very wrong of him. Not that I am* not *making fun of the regent, since I'm writing the story. But that's different. Don't ask why. Shut up or I'll stop typing right now, I mean it —*

The regent's entourage (that's him and everyone with him) marched across the square and down a wide street. A crowd of people, visitors to Scrofula, followed. Bogbrush could tell they weren't local Scrofulans because they looked and spoke differently. Some were buying brightly colored garments inscribed with slogans such as "My Granny Went to Scrofula and All I Got Was this Lousy T-shirt." A group of men and women from the eastern lands wore wax tablets to draw pictures of all the sights they came to. Pale families from the Foggy Islands complained about the food because it wasn't exactly like what they ate at home, which was famously horrible. A couple from the western grasslands of Chixas were loudly comparing the three-thousand-year-old sacred temples of Scrofula to new buildings in their homeland (which were, they decided, bigger, cleaner and generally better than the old stuff littering the ancient streets of Scrofula).

"Honeybunch, this place is a real dump! Everything's old and tiny!" declared the woman from Chixas. "Sure it is, sweetcakes!" replied her husband. "But we have to travel the world so we'll know just how great Chixas is!" Then they both made a noise that sounded like an unhappy donkey, and everyone around took a step away from them.

"Ruddy tourists," grumbled Sneaky as he stopped the cart by a machine marked "Parking, one copper piece per hour." Sneaky reached into a passing tourist's pocket and pulled out a handful of change to put in the meter. Diphtheria jumped down off the wagon, Bogbrush fell off Nobby's back and the three of them followed the tourists on foot. Nobby wanted to come, too, but the barbarian tied him to the cart, much against his will. Sneaky stole a carrot from a passing vegetable vendor ("Cabbage Bill's Deluxe Root Veggies — None Rootier") and gave it to the pony as a treat. As you can tell, he liked to keep up his thieving skills.

> *TOURISTS are visitors who arrive to buy tacky souvenirs, get pictures made of themselves with stupid expressions on their faces standing next to ancient monuments and complain about the food, which isn't what they eat at home. People don't like to admit that they are tourists, but they think that everyone else around them is a tourist.*

"It's this way to some temple with a wood axe in a big rock," said Mr. Chixas to his wife, loud enough that Bogbrush could hear them a hundred paces away. "The guidebook says something about a True King being able to haul the axe out."

"You should give it a try, honey," replied his wife. "You could carry it in the axe rack in your wagon." Sneaky pulled a face, Diphtheria rolled her eyes and Bogbrush wondered where he could get an axe rack of his own.

The regent and his procession passed through an archway toward a building even older than the others, with ornately carved columns and blocks of marble. As Bogbrush saw it, a voice came into his head. It told him that this ancient temple, all chiseled stones and engraved gold, must indeed have been the place where the last True King had left his axe stuck in a rock. It was a mystical voice.

"It says here on page fourteen, Mildred, 'The Shrine of the Axe.' Some old king stuck a chopper in a bit o' rock. What'd he do that for, d'you think?"

Bogbrush looked behind him, where a tourist was waving a guidebook at her friend. She wasn't mystical at all.

CHAPTER 20-13

(Now wait – is that right?)

The temple was packed, mostly with tourists. Some drew the scene on wax tablets or wrote to their relatives on the back of something called "post-slabs." Others chewed on delicacies offered by Cabbage Bill; his cauliflower-in-a-bun seemed especially popular with the audience.

Bogbrush was taller than anyone else (except a camel that had wandered in), so he could see over the crowd. The regent was seated on a splendid throne, his cronies and sycophants gathered around him trying to look dignified and important. An ancient priest, white robed and white bearded, sat beside him.

WORDS OF THE DAY — *A double helping of grammatical fun!*

crony — *you have friends. That obnoxious kid who makes fun of you has cronies. See the difference? Your friends are wonderful people, his are jerks for hanging around with him.*

sycophant — *one who sucks up. It's Greek. Fancy words are often Greek in origin, like* psychiatry, diagnosis *and* lug nut.

In front of them was a huge axe, planted in a massive block of granite as casually as if it was stuck in a log for the fire.

When I say massive, the only thing I can immediately compare it to is a garbage truck, only this is a fantasy tale, and fantasy tales don't feature garbage trucks. I think elves take out the trash or something. So scrub that comparison. But you get the idea how big this hard, heavy boulder was.

Bogbrush was in awe to be present at last in the famous Shrine of the Axe, the place the priestess of Belch had spoken of. He was impressed by the solemn dignity of the occasion. "That is a very big axe," he boomed, "in a very big rock. I hast never seeneth such a very big axe in such a very big rock." Someone in the crowd snickered.

"Shh!" said Diphtheria.

"Shut up!" whispered Sneaky. "Let's see what 'appens."

GOOD ADVICE: *There will be many times in life where the best thing you can do is "shut up and see what happens." A wise man once said it is better to stay quiet and let people think you might be an idiot than to open your mouth and definitely prove you are an idiot.*

The ancient priest tottered to his feet and mumbled something into his beard for several minutes. Then the regent arose and began to speak.

"Citizens of Scwofula," he began. Bogbrush started to giggle, but Diphtheria elbowed him in the arm.

"Citizens *and* touwists to our gweat city," continued the regent. "Welcome to the Shwine of the Axe. Today we celebwate the cewemony of the Axe in the Stone. Many years ago our beloved wuler left this mighty axe stuck in this wugged fwagment of wock. Alas, the king was never seen aftew that day. My gweat-gweat-gwandfather had to step in and take contwol of Scwofula as the first weegent. Nobody weally knows what fate befell his glowious majesty. But the legend wuns like this: one day the Twue King will wetuwn and weign. We will know the Twue King when he takes the gweat axe out of the wugged wock. Of course, as weegent I look fowward to casting aside all these dweadful wesponsiblities of wuling, and wetiring to Flowida. But, until that time, I wemain wesponsible."

The regent gave a big sigh, as if riding around in a sedan chair and being fed peeled grapes was a terrible effort, which only his strong sense of duty allowed him to carry on despite the hardships of the job. He continued.

"Evewy year at this cewemony, anyone who claims the wight to twy to waise the weapon has his chance. Does any man claim that wight?"

Diphtheria bristled that only men were allowed to try, even though she thought it was all a ridiculous joke. Nobody could possibly pull that axe out of the stone.

A man stepped forward.

CHAPTER 20-14

(Must be right, surely?)

No, not *that* man. Another bloke.

Bogbrush was still taking the "shut up and see what happens" advice when a fellow stepped out of the crowd to take his turn. He was dressed in a king's crown and a purple robe with fancy borders at the neck and sleeves.

Diphtheria sniffed. "That crown's not real. I know where to buy 'em for five copper pieces. And the robe's just a dressing gown with some stitching. He's just trying to dress the part."

The "king" marched over to the great stone. The crowd went silent. A drummer began beating his tom-tom. Then, as he reached a final thump, the monarch-in-a-dressing-gown pulled at the axe handle. The crowd gasped.

The axe did not budge. The "king" tugged and pulled

until his face was red. He gasped deeply and tried some more. He failed again; his eyes bulged with the effort. His breathing was hard. The man seemed almost ready to take the handle in his teeth and gnaw on it when the soldiers stepped forward and led him away by the elbows.

The crowd laughed uproariously, and there was a round of applause for the apparently-not-the-actual-king's efforts. Some people admired his pluck, but most just thought he was an idiot. Bogbrush would have agreed with both sentiments (he approved of pluck, and felt a kindred spirit with all idiots), but he had more important things on his mind. It was he, Bogbrush, grandson of Bumrash, son of Dad, who would be the True King in just a few moments!

WORD OF THE DAY: pluck *is an old-fashioned word that means "courage." You'll find it used in ancient, moldy British novels where spirited youths of a century ago take on bullies, Zulu warriors and opposing cricket teams. Your author (me) read all those books as a child in the 1890s and likes the word a lot.*

The same word is used concerning the pulling out of unsightly hairs, among other meanings.

The regent stood up. "Alas," he said (as if he thought it was a real shame that he had to go on eating the peeled grapes), "our contestant appeaws to be mewely a pwetender, not the Twue King." He scanned the crowd. "Anyone else want to give it a twy?"

There was a sort of collective head shake from the audience. Even the man from Chixas (whom Bogbrush understood to be named Sugar-Pie Honeybunch) seemed to think that maybe he shouldn't stand up and make a complete fool of himself in front of two hundred complete strangers and his wife, Sweetcakes.

"Oh, well," said the regent. "In that case I shall just have to cawwy on until next yeaw. What a weight of wesponsibility!" He sighed again.

"Not so fast!" shouted Bogbrush. "I claim the right to heft the axe with my mighty thews!"

The regent looked at Bogbrush, all muscles and veins and general hugeness.

"Ah, well, we've weally finished up hewe. Pewhaps next time —" he muttered.

"No!" boomed the ancient priest, surprising everyone around him. "The legend says that all who wish to try must be permitted their chance." He turned a fierce eyebrow toward the regent. "He must make his attempt!"

The crowd roared in agreement. Most of them had thoroughly enjoyed seeing the man with the fake crown and dressing gown gasping and heaving at the axe handle. If some other half-wit wanted to make a fool of himself, that was worth staying to watch. The regent looked unhappy as he sized up Bogbrush, but he could hardly declare that there was a rule saying that only contenders of small stature and feeble strength were allowed to try. The old priest would know better than that.

"Do your best!" cried Diphtheria.

"Get ready to slip out the back door," Sneaky whispered. "If anyone asks, we don't know 'im." But Bogbrush didn't hear that part.

He strode toward the massive hunk of granite.

The audience quieted down as they watched the young barbarian giant square up before the axe. Mildred and her friend — the girls with the guidebook — giggled and went "Ooooh" as Bogbrush flexed his muscles. Two men started laying bets as to whether this big fellow could haul the axe out of the rock. Somebody came around selling hot dogs on a stick. (They weren't actual dogs, although they may once have been rats.)

Okay, the audience wasn't all that quiet. But they were very, very interested in what would happen next.

CHAPTER 20-15
(Gotta be right, right?)

"Who awt thou?" demanded the regent.

"I shall tell thee once I have hoisted yon chopper!" replied Bogbrush.

The crowd liked that one. So did Sneaky. "A witty retort! A snappy comeback! I'd never 'ave thought the lad could come up with one of those."

"Well, actually he didn't," replied Diphtheria. "He and I have been practicing that line every day for the last week."

Bogbrush took hold of the axe handle. He flexed his mighty muscles. The drummer began tom-tomming a sharp, slow beat. The crowd hushed. Bogbrush had a look of concentration (which appeared a lot like constipation) on his face.

With a flourish of beats, the drummer stopped.

Bogbrush pulled. The veins in his arms stood out. Sweat glistened on his forehead. His eyeballs almost popped out.

And then he lifted the axe.

The crowd went wild — jabbering, hollering and arguing about the bets they'd just made. Diphtheria shrieked and grabbed Sneaky's arm in amazement. For a brief moment Sneaky stopped picking the pocket of the man in front of him and gaped at his huge friend's astonishing achievement. "Good lad,

Bogbrush," he muttered, then went back to the serious business of stealing the man's wallet.

TAKE YOUR WORK SERIOUSLY! Note how Sneaky, a professional petty thief, continues with his work even though there is a distraction. He concentrates. He puts forth an effort. Isn't that what your parents and teachers have been telling you to do?

The regent turned white, and his entourage had the look of guests about to be thrown out of the banquet.

"Thank you, citizens of Scrofula!" boomed Bogbrush. "I am your rightful ruler, your True King, as you can see from this axe in my hands." He hoisted the weapon even higher above his head. "The first three … six … two … things I decree are —"

"You 'aven't pulled it out of the stone!" shouted one of the True King's new subjects. "It don't count!"

Everyone pointed and jabbered at Bogbrush. He looked up. He knew he was holding the axe aloft.

What he hadn't realized was that he was also holding the rock. The axe was still firmly wedged into the granite block.

Nobody had ever, ever lifted anything so big and heavy. But, as Sneaky was to say later on, that wasn't the point, was it?

The audience suddenly stopped their shrieking, yelling and general uproariousness. But the ones who were pointing did so with greater pointiness, and others pointed for the first time. It seemed to Bogbrush that they were trying to tell him something.

Not the bit about the rock. He'd already got that.

A **C-R-A-C-K** came from above him. It sounded

woody. Like splintering wood. Like, say, for example, an axe handle breaking in two.

Oh.

CHAPTER 279

(Just messing about!)

LET'S START WITH SOME PHYSICS! If I were a science teacher I'd have some sort of complicated formula or equation here, explaining the relationship between

1) weight (as in a big huge mammajamma lump or rock) and

2) mass (that same bit of rock) dropping from a height of, say, above Bogbrush's head (which is something to do with kinetic energy, I think, but I failed my physics exams every time), and there'd be other stuff about exactly how it works.

But I'm not a science teacher.

The axe handle shattered and the rock fell. Now, as we've said, this was a very big rock. Garbage-truck big, as I told you earlier. (Pay attention, this might be on the test.)

It smashed into the marble floor, destroying a three-thousand-year-old tile mosaic of the founding of Scrofula. It careened sideways into gold statues of the first nine kings of the city and battered them into a heap of broken arms and legs. It crashed into marble columns, and they fell, knocking down other marble columns. An altar fell over, more or less because it wanted to join in the fun, and some curtains caught fire when a candlestick took a dive, like an Italian soccer star.

It was a worse mess than your teenage sister's room.

The crowd bolted for the doors, windows and a gap where a whole section of wall had fallen down. The regent and his entourage were trapped on the stage and held scrolls and hats and umbrellas over their heads to protect them from giant rocks.

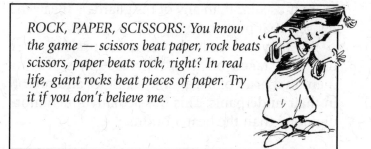

ROCK, PAPER, SCISSORS: You know the game — scissors beat paper, rock beats scissors, paper beats rock, right? In real life, giant rocks beat pieces of paper. Try it if you don't believe me.

Even Bogbrush realized that things weren't going the way he hoped they would.

The regent stood up. He was covered in dust, and his almost-a-crown was bent into a sad, doggie-toy shape. Nevertheless, he had a lot to say.

"Guawds! Awwest that man at once! Clap him in iwons!"

The guards had all been hiding under the fallen altar. Guards know when to hide.

Bogbrush brandished the broken axe handle at them in a menacing sort of way. Actually it was a confused sort of way, but they all decided it was menacing. They ran away, bolting like bunnies in the presence of a puppy.

"They've probably gone to fetch reinforcements," said Diphtheria. She used her Sarcastic Tone when she said this.

"Yeah," agreed Sneaky, in his own Sarcastic Tone. "There's only ten of 'em. They need at least an 'undred to take on our lad Bogbrush."

The regent watched them flee, then called upon his sedan chair bearers (who were much bigger and more muscular than any of his guards). "Beawers! Awwest that pwetender!"

But they'd already departed themselves. They had each taken off their silly costumes, leaving them in a heap of baggy silky thingies and run off in their underpants. This was actually much more dignified than the bearer outfits.

Which left the regent on his own, except for the ancient priest. All the cronies and hangers-on had hangered off. He stamped his foot and stuck it through a very large portrait of his own great-great-grandfather, which had hung above the altar until, well, about forty-five seconds previously. "I weally must pwotest at this destwuction —" he began.

"Am I king yet?" demanded Bogbrush. He wasn't sure how the rules worked. "I'm going to see if I can shake the rock off yon axe. Wilt that count, then?"

This was a good question, *in theory*, if you really wanted to decide the rules. But what actually happened was this …

THE LAST CHAPTER!!!

**(Well done! You got this far.
Are you being paid to read this?)**

Bogbrush reached down and, with a mighty grab of the broken axe — really just the end of the handle stuck into the axe head, and hardly anything to take hold of — he hoisted the rock into the air and shook it.

This was a mighty deed, indeed, and yet a very silly thing to do.

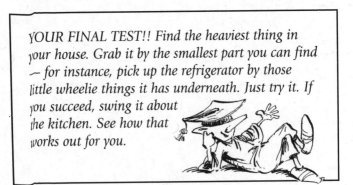

YOUR FINAL TEST!! Find the heaviest thing in your house. Grab it by the smallest part you can find — for instance, pick up the refrigerator by those little wheelie things it has underneath. Just try it. If you succeed, swing it about the kitchen. See how that works out for you.

Uh-huh. That's what happened.

The rock hurtled through the air. The regent dived for safety. The old priest ducked. Sneaky and Diphtheria ducked as well, even though they were already hunched down behind Bogbrush. The rock missed them all.

Instead, it smashed into the biggest, thickest, oldest pillar standing. And then it wasn't standing anymore. With a creak and a crack and then the noise that makes everyone want to yell **"TIMBERRRRRR!!!!!"** it fell over. The roof above it decided to join it on the ground, and the walls agreed with the plan. There was deafening noise, immense clouds of dust and then — silence.

Diphtheria raised her head. Sneaky poked up from under a column. The regent, covered in white dust, was sitting in the broken remains of his sedan chair. His crown was completely bent. The ancient priest was even whiter than before.

Bogbrush stood in the center of it all. His giant muscles were coated with dirt, his helmet was crushed flat (again), and let's just say it was lucky he'd been wearing his chain-mail underwear. Flying rock splinters are sharp.

He had one question.

"Can I have another try?"

The ancient priest shook his head.

"Oh," said Bogbrush, looking slightly disappointed. "I suppose I be not the True King, then. My quest is over. Still, I expecteth another one will come along in a little while."

"Quests are like buses that way," said the ancient priest. As I mentioned earlier, nobody had invented buses yet, so the others just thought he was old and a bit mad.

Sneaky had already snuck away, hoping the gents'

room had survived the destruction. His bladder could stand only so much excitement.

The old priest and the regent (now sobbing tears of rage) stood among the ruins, facing the giant barbarian and the singer/actress/research alchemist. Everyone was covered in dust. Everything was broken. Nobody could think of anything else to say. Probably the guards would come back after a bit (perhaps with reinforcements), and Diphtheria didn't want to be around when they did. It really was time to leave. "Come on, Bogbrush!" she called out. "Let's go before we get into any more trouble."

"Ho!" replied Bogbrush. "Trouble is my friend."